DOUBTING
THOMAS

DOUBTING THOMAS

KAT RICKER

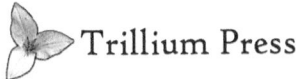 Trillium Press

Thank you to my father, Tom and Christine.

Cover photo   Christine Ferreira
Editor   John C. Ricker
Production   Tom Sumner

©2010 Trillium Press
www.MightyKat.net
ISBN 978-0-615-31849-3

*Dedicated to critical thinkers and
old-school Catholics everywhere.*

Believe nothing, no matter who has said it,
not even if I have said, unless it agrees with
your own reason and your own common sense.

—Buddha

Of course, I am sworn to secrecy in all things I am told in the confessional. But I believe it is all right to repeat these things in my own confession. He was the strongest fortifier of my faith, and he came at a time when I was in need of fortification.

It was the week before Lent began. The lines for confession were very long, and I remember thinking that these were the people who wanted to say their confession before the seasonal rush began, with intentions of keeping themselves clean until the lines shortened up again. I had opened the church early and lighted the candles, unlocking the confessional and laying out my thin stole. I knelt for a while at the side altar of the Blessed Mother, trying to pray, but instead thinking how the paint was technically uneven in the eyes, the inner corner of the right hanging slightly lower than the left. It wasn't much; hardly anyone would ever notice. But for those who did, it was a distraction. More than that, really; it was a real drawback, a mar in the otherwise phenomenal beauty of the church, and whoever had painted it should have kept it closer in mind. It was almost insulting to be expected to find inspiration through an imagistic vessel painted by some stooped foreign worker making five cents an hour, cranking out as many sidelong glances from divinity as could be mustered in the last hour before hitting the bar. The whole idea irritated me to such a point that I didn't even realize it when four of the back rows became spotted with people, all spacing themselves out for privacy, yet all sitting in the same section. I rose from my musings and prepared my confessional.

For the first hour and a half, they were all predictable and undiverting. Two reports of gluttony, some lustful desires, a handful of unpaid debts, and a silo of cursings. If I had even one parishioner who didn't take the name of the Lord in vain, I think I'd send his mailing address to the pope. So the evening passed, until him.

The door opened and was carefully closed, the kneeler silent, not realizing the slight weight.

"Bless me Father, for I have sinned. It has been two weeks since my last confession."

It was a young voice, but it had some presence. It seemed naturally subdued, as if in outside life he preferred not to use it if given the option, and as he told his small sins, his precision in speaking became apparent. He used the minimal amount of words necessary, and, if seeking a word, allowed himself long draughts of silence to find it. I found him easy to listen to, and in some subtle way he commanded my attention. And there was a comfort there. I remember thinking what a trite idea it was, but that nevertheless, with his youth and his wan, high voice, he exuded a certain goodness that pleased me. His confession had been menial enough, as most boys' are, and it wasn't until I told him his penance that the unusual began. I assigned him to say a rosary, and guide his thoughts toward the Lord's way, as I tell most.

"But, Father, is that enough?"

"Enough? Well, is there something else that you would like to do?"

"It just seems, small, when I know how sinful I am."

"What should you do?"

"You would know, Father. I would not contradict you. But with your permission, I will ask Him."

"Ask whom?"

"The Lord."

"Oh, of course. You ask Him, and then do whatever you feel is necessary. But you will leave here with my absolution." I moved forward and held up my hand. "I absolve you of your sins, in the name of the Father and of the Son and of the Holy Spirit. Amen."

He made his Act of Contrition in an impressively heart-felt tone.

"Your sins are forgiven. Go in peace and sin no more." I closed the little window.

☦

He was back the next week. Again, the silence of his weightlessness on the kneeler, and the shy, distant voice.

"Bless me, Father, for I have sinned. It has been one week since my last confession."

"Go ahead."

"The penance, Father. It was not enough. My soul is black. I said the rosary, and then I said another. I said them for a few days."

"Yes?"

"It didn't relieve my conscience; so I asked Him what to do. He told me what he wanted, but he also said that I should tell you, Father, that it isn't enough, what you give as penance. He has more demand before His pardon is granted."

I shifted so as not to miss a word.

"My son, please explain to me how it is that you have talked with Him."

He was quiet for a moment. I think my question confused him, as an adult who wonders how to explain the obvious. "We talk."

I backtracked. "What did He want from you as penance?"

"Blood."

"I don't understand. What do you mean, blood?"

"Not that my blood is worth anything, of course. That's not what I mean. But it pleases Him, to have this small sacrifice."

"And how did you fill this penance?"

He was quiet again, longer this time.

"As a priest, I am asking that you tell me how you fulfilled this penance."

The silence seemed tighter, and I wasn't sure how to proceed.

"Son, -"

It was too late. I heard the confessional door close behind him.

⁜

I wasn't sure exactly what it was that I had on my hands. Mentally disturbed? Attention-seeking? He filled my thoughts the next morning at the rectory breakfast, and Hilda took note of my distraction, as she most scrupulously takes note of all things.

"Got your mail in for today, and Brian Hobbs would like to speak to you about Thursday's meeting. Give him a call as soon as possible."

"Thank-you."

She poured more coffee into my cup.

"And how were confessions?"

"Twenty-five, maybe. Not bad for this time of the year."

"No, not at all. Are you done with that section?"

I passed her the grocery section of the newspaper and sipped my coffee. I like a good strong cup of coffee first thing in the morning. I take it black. Black. Black as a soul.

⁜

A funeral, wedding interview, several lunches with

4

area diplomats for this and the other... The week passed inconsequently enough. The women preparing the church for Lent were in a constant flurry about flower ordering and the like.

I wondered where he'd come from. Not that the city was so small that I could be expected to know everyone in it, but it still seemed odd that he should appear out of nowhere. Perhaps the family had just moved into the area.

He wasn't in confessions the next week, and I more or less forgot about him in the beginning of the Lenten season. Everyone wanted attention, and it exhausted me. Purple banners were being erected, and the local paper was doing a feature on area Lenten preparations; overall, if people weren't clamoring for public notice within the church, they were seeking it by means of the church. I wondered how many were actually working on spiritual preparation for the season.

In preparation for evening vespers, I entered the church after sunset, entering through the back into the sacristy. I gathered the candle lighter and wooden matches to light the candles on the sanctuary. I was startled to find a small figure kneeling at the rail of the side altar, and further surprised that it was a young boy. I set about the routine as usual, genuflecting and walking across the marble floor to the tall unlit beeswax columns. I was peakedly intrigued, wondering immediately whether this was the same boy from the confessional. No reason that it should be, I reasoned, but the possibility demanded more and more of my thoughts. I stole a glance at the boy. About the age befitting the voice, perhaps twelve or thirteen, light sandy hair with a cowlick, something of a Norman Rockwell subject, he seemed completely oblivious to me or anything else. His eyes were closed and hands clasped in fervent prayer, mouth closed. I had to tend to the candles on that side of the altar anyway, and so I moved carefully over, trying deliberately not to look at him. His skin seemed to shine in the candlelight. Yes, it was actually shining because he was sweating, sweating profusely in fact. His face seemed placid enough, and yet his small hands were moving. They were trembling. I wondered whether his clothes were damp from the perspiration, and thought they perhaps appeared so, but in the low light I couldn't be sure. My left hand suddenly grew very warm, in fact hot, and I jerked it away from the tip of a flame. I crossed back into the sacristy feeling embarrassed.

At the end of vespers, I heard myself announce that there would be confessions directly after vespers. It all makes perfect sense, I thought. Many people can't wait the long lines of regular Lent confessions.

"Bless me, Father, for I have sinned. I really sinned. I—I ran out of my last confession."

"God will be glad that you have returned. Why did you run?"

"Because it was all going to start again."

"What was?"

His voice sounded earnestly distraught. "You wanted to know things. You were going to ask about our conversations and what I see. I would tell you, and then the horrible things would begin."

"What things?"

A note of helplessness toned his voice. "You wouldn't understand, or maybe believe me. Then I couldn't come here anymore."

"My son," I began. (This had always seemed a false address to me, I resented it when used on me as a boy and never used it myself until now. I wasn't trying to draw him out with it or any such nonsense; the words just seemed very natural with him.) "It is my job to understand. I will understand things that others don't. Feel free to say anything here. I do not judge. God does."

·✠·

The visions started when he was five, or so he articulated

them at that age. Nights he would wake screaming from an otherwise silent night, inconsolable by either parent, who both invariably ran flapping down the hall, hearts gripped by the urgency and pure terror of his screams.

These fits left him too weak to stand, yet flaying wildly, entangling himself in the blankets nearly to the brink of suffocation at times. Sometimes his hysteria allowed some coherence, and then it was always the same.

"The Devil. He wanted me again, he laughed at me, and he threatened to throw hot coals and burn my skin until I was as black as he, and I couldn't run, I couldn't get away. . . " Although there were many variations, it was always a form of the Devil, and no amount of talking could convince him that it hadn't been real. Fortunately, these episodes threw him into a solid sleep quickly afterward that carried him into late morning, although the rest of the household could not boast such effects.

The doctor pronounced it a hyperactive imagination run amuck without a definable trigger or cure, and prescribed a very mild sedative, with much reserve at that.

More than once his father had sat up late nights trying to relieve him of another complaint, the incessant singing of birds or grandiose music. This drew slightly more conversation from the pediatrician, who mentioned that Virginia Woolf had described similar disturbances. But the final conclusion was that once again, the boy's mind overworked itself. Early wind downs and quiet evenings were recommended.

In school he was a model student, quiet and obedient, following through every homework assignment. He was the one whom teachers would trustingly send to the office on errands or let pass out test papers. Basically a loner, he did not involve himself in any extracurricular activities and walked the lengthy walk home after school instead of taking the available bus.

He wouldn't talk much about his past, but I inferred from

7

the little that he did say that his visions had interfered with his school life at the Catholic School for the Enlightened in Minnesota to such an extent that the attention of the local priest was sought, who pronounced him a rare subject of demonic visitation. This must have been a small and backward town, for whatever ruckus was raised was enough for the family to pull up stakes and move here. Although he was reluctant to talk about these topics, he would talk at length about the visions, if I prodded him, when he at last felt that I could be trusted.

He felt little pride about them. On the contrary, they filled him with fear, both from the specifically fear-inspiring messages from the Devil and the sometimes sterner ones of the Lord. He was terrified of being discovered in his secret and because of its intensity felt strong enough to be obvious at any moment to the onlooking world. Indeed, the whole involvement, which predominated his thoughts, seemed much more a source of misery to him than anything else. I felt pity for him.

But, he assured me, at other times the joy of union with the Lord was so exquisite, so acute an ecstasy, that he would gladly lie down his life in such moments, for no greater bliss could here ever be known.

Minnesota

He picked up his mother's sewing needle. The light fell smoothly through the eye, glinting along the straight line of silver that lay between his fingers. He turned it in his palm, slipped it into his pocket, and left the room.

The summer heat remained thick in the night, the grass stiff under his bare feet. The crush of darkened green and brown led him to the toolshed in the back of the cemetery. He dislodged the mass of bramble and limb he'd pressed to the rear wall, followed the dents of structure up to the window, and climbed inside. The air was oppressive with traces of staled incense and the breaths of old wood.

Genuflection. The candles came to life under his care, two diagonal racks of four tapers, joining the light of the perpetual beeswax log staring from its red glass holder. He lit the censure, releasing coils of frankincense and sandalwood. One by one, his clothes came off, t-shirt, jeans, underpants. His small form stood naked except for the scapular hung over his chest and back, shadows showing him small and knobbily underweight. Bending under even his slight weight, the cracking board bridged over brick stacks bit into his knees and roughed against his skin, chafing the hardened flesh. Lips caressed whispers, edges of muted prayer lifting into the quietude. The tall ceramic Sacred Heart statue stared down at him, the shine of enamel become sad, brown tiny eyes of wounded desperation and shattered love. He'd seen similar eyes on the covers of romance novels, massive emotion crying in the aisles of supermarkets and newsstand corners.

Overtaking the bench he faced was a wide collection of devotional items; small, square cards framing Christ among lambs; Christ, the Bearer of Mercies flowing through the paper with an upraised hand forming the sign of peace, two rays of light emitting from his blindingly white heart region; Christ slumped over a broad, flat rock in an expression of muted resignation. A large black rosary lay coiled and waiting in an emptied tin cannister. The bench was otherwise filled with small odds gathered nicely in his short amount of lifetime.

He pressed his lips to the floor, laying prostrate on the warm, packed earth. After a time, his gaze lifted, his eyes meeting the eyes of the statue. The face of Christ held wordlessly still, abject reserve, unwavering ceramic. The boy's eyes began to move, not through any will of his own, a mounting pull feeling as if each eye was torn in a different direction, his focus growing blurred and soft, shadows pooling in spots of vision, ebbing, shrinking, like water on a quivering leaf.

The face softened, becoming pliant and removed from itself, as if clay was replaced with air, and shape, and form. The eyes grew in intensity, deepening in their stare, reaching straight into his very soul. He knew he was laid bare now. Nothing was hidden at all. He knew the sensation of lowering his head without moving, a shelf of consciousness stepped down in humility. The brown eyes steeped to black, taking over the face, floating out of the murky fog of background. A sudden shining wave of hair. Patch of white robe. Yes, he knew, white was the light of his Lord. White was His and His only, white was his dominion and domain.

With enormous effort, he moved his frozen hand to his side. His small, stiff fingers curled round the sliver of silver he'd brought and drew it toward him, catching glints of the candles. Keeping his eyes fastened on the Christ eyes, the boy put his hands before him in an attitude of offering. Christ waited with infinite patience as the boy placed his hands together, one pinching the needle, one flat. The connection with Christ surged a sudden wave through his body, and he pricked his fingertip, feeling the sharp shoot of pain, watching the rounded dome of red gather and swell on top of his skin. He sighed. Christ was warm.

The boy pushed his life out before the infinite eyes, offering the dark skeletal framework of his existence, a mite in the grandeur in his midst. He saw it before him, not lingering too long on the vision, lest he displace his mind and create some pride where none was deserved, and sent it toward the open arms of Christ, up through the viscous passage that parted them, growing paler and paler in the washing of His light until his lids quivered too violently, snapping down a curtain on his vision, severing the tunnel that had been formed. His neck let go with the new darkness, his blonde head hitting the dirt floor with a loud force. He was still. Breath began to find its way inside in short, shallow spurts, the thin ribs wrapping his lungs working with involuntary ferocity. Consciousness spilled from the boy as fluid running from a wound.

"our shirts are in the back laundry room. Been a bit of a back-up lately. I told you that mustard stain wouldn't come out."

"Thank-you, Hilda. I'll remember next time."

"Quiet today, Father. Sunny day out there." She finished reheating my coffee from an orange pot, overlooking my involuntary grimace. I'd told her I didn't want decaf.

"They'll be cleaning your room this morning. And Regina would like to speak to you about the accounting before you go."

"Well, I'm here. I haven't got any place to –"

"Yes, you do. Petersons would like to talk to you about enrolling their son in the school."

"Petersons?"

She pushed an apple danish at me. "New parishioners, this year. From Minnesota."

Minnesota

His hands were like cat's paws. The palms held a soft, cushy callousness, the skin silky and impenetrable. His mother snatched them up in her own.

"Tommy, wake up. Wake up." His eyes flickered but remained unopened. "Tommy, wake up now. I need to talk to you." They rolled toward her, in the attitude of utter and complete blankness that only premature jarring can produce. She shoved his hands toward his face. "What's wrong with your hands, Tommy? What've you been doing?" He blinked. "Tommy, I am asking you a question. What is wrong with your hands?"

"Don't worry, Mother. My hands are fine."

She lurched into his face, shaking his palms in hers with each word for emphasis. "Thomas, I am asking you a question, and you will give me an acceptable answer. Now, for the last time, what have you done to your hands?"

He considered them. "Well, Mother, they must have gotten burned."

She struck him. "How?"

"I guess I was using the stove in the dark last night."

"And you had no idea your hands were on fire?"

"Well, Mother, even if I did, I wouldn't wake you and Daddy. You see, I'm all right now, and we could all still be sleeping until the morning."

She struck him again. "Your father won't be getting much sleep tonight, Thomas."

⊹

The Doctor on call in the emergency room filled his coffee cup, left it behind the nurses' station to cool, and went between the next divider curtains. A man had hemorrhaged badly in the night, and was in a sedate but extreme state of discomfiture. The doctor finished the exam and began writing the orders for overnight admission. As he pushed his pen through the inevitable illegible loops and scrawls, he overheard voices from the next sector.

"I can't take this nonsense from him anymore, Leonard. I've had it. If you think you can handle him, then you stay home and watch him 24 hours a day. I can't do this anymore. Last time it was the ankle binding. Now this. He's going to kill himself, and you just won't look at it. I can't do it anymore, Leonard." He finished the papers and moved round to look at the lovely disheveled owner of the voice.

"Good evening. What have we here?"

The man stepped toward him in gawky gait. "Hi, I'm Lawrence Peterson, and this is Sherri Peterson. This is our son Tommy. He seems to have burned his hands."

The small boy looked at him in a wan, steady gaze. The doctor squared up his shoulders and strode to the railed bedside. "Well, let's have a look. You certainly have burned your hands. How did this happen?"

No response. The mother moved in.

"He's been into the stove tonight. "

"Have you? And what were doing in the stove?"

"I wasn't in the stove. I was working at the stovetop. I was melting some candlewax down to make more candles."

"A young boy like you?" He checked himself and looked at the parents, who were reacting in degrees of embarrassment. The woman finally spoke.

"You never know what he's going to get into." They regarded one another. The doctor broke with professional urgency and began writing on his clipboard.

"I'd like him to stay for burn treatment and observation. These burns are serious. If they had been much worse, he could very well have done permanent damage, possibly lost his hands. As it is, they will be scarred." He glanced at the boy, startled to find the vaguest, but most definite, light of a smile. Weirdos, he thought. He tore off a sheet and handed it to Leonard with a pen. Coffee.

✛

He came home with bandages on his hands. His mother drove him from the hospital, caught up in the new tact of over-niceness. She pushed into his silence with obvious attempts at comradery, broken, garishly pitched lines of weather and mild gossip. He stared out the window, his mouth a straight line, hands folded into his lap, bearing out the ride.

✛

The statue had waited. He reached out his arms, displaying the white wrapped stumps on his wrists, holding them out straight, long after the evening shadows turned to the curtains of night, closing velvet shackles round the oratory. He slipped into the stare, waiting for the transfiguring of the eyes. Slowly, it emerged, the strange form of life which belonged only to this moment, glowing from the idol. The eyes receded, the jaw slackened; he watched, unflinching, waiting out this new shift. A blurring of red raised the heart out from the image, darkness isolating the thorned, bursting organ in midair. It hovered and grew, commanding the boy's every attention, burning away all the layers of his mind, all the thoughts he'd had went leaping into the furnace blazing brightly in the Lord's omniscience and falling, destroyed, into little pops and explosions, dancing round the heart, a tarantella of his humanness ringing the immortal. All the thoughts perished save one, a hard, tiny black one. It wavered under the wound for a moment, three drops of blood welling, growing heavy, and falling over the black disgrace, rinsing it in the holy blood. Suddenly, with speeding thrust, it flew into the boy's own heart, hitting with a stinging dart that sent him reeling, backwards, falling onto the flat dirt floor.

His faith was extraordinary. Beyond extraordinary. As Lent began, I witnessed the most personal relationship I have ever known between a person and Christ in His final suffering. The boy's voice grew heavy and hollow as he spoke of Jesus' pain, the sharp and drawn-out dread of the doom which He knew awaited Him, though no others could, and the sorrow at the decadence in man's soul. Fridays found him most removed from this world, as is typical of those with a special connection with Christ. I mentioned to him once during a confession that Theresa Neuman lost five to eight pounds every Friday, in concurrence with regular visions. Already distant from this world and the way conversations run within it, his voice here took off into a sort of chant, a rapid and subdued monotone.

"Theresa Neumann, suffered severe illness all her life. Once the abilities to walk and to see were restored, the Lord visited her in visions of His Passion. For many years she neither ate nor drank, and rarely slept."

I tried to acknowledge this, but he didn't seem aware of my voice.

""These visions before long were accompanied by physical signs on her own body: blood streamed from her side and from her eyes; marks corresponding to a crown of thorns appeared upon her head; a red bruise, not actually bleeding, but oozing blood, appeared upon her right shoulder as though from the angular weight of a heavy burden; weals, as though from scourging, covered her body; and the stigmata appeared in her hands and feet. Here, in the place of nails, pieces of hard flesh, like plugs, filled the holes. . . After the climax of the Good Friday's vision, when she has watched Christ's body droop upon the Cross, and her own body has drooped with it, her mouth falling half open, her limbs relaxed and motionless, her heart for five minutes actually ceases to beat.""

Eagle and the Hawk, p. 171

He kept talking, in the same quick, streaming manner, but his voice trailed into such quiet that I could no longer make out what he was saying. I tried gently to rouse him, but in a few moments, all that was to be heard was his breathing, in long, heavy draughts, exhales of exhaustion. While I knew him to be asleep, I knelt and began a rosary.

Minnesota

The straightrazor felt heavy in his hands. He stared at the portrait of the Sacred Heart on his lap, infusing his humbleness into the warm sadness of the dark charcoaled eyes. The face in the picture looked to him, it changed with subtle shifts of expression that called an even greater sadness from the boy, twisted like a braid with the exquisite joy of the recognition in the eyes, the silent communication that was being granted him.

He smoothed the oil onto his palm. Oil like the holy oil mixed with the sacred blood, oil as holy oil, oil as essence, essence of holiness. It had been blessed, this oil, blessed and come all the way from Fatima. He stared into the eyes without blinking. *Oil for your wounds*, he thought. *Would that I could have balmed them myself.* He brought the oil to his head and pulled his hands slowly over his head, the golden locks becoming pliant and thick under his wet touch. The eyes watched him, never leaving his own eyes, becoming lighter with an ethereal glow. Sweet, undeserved approval. He raked his fingers carefully through each strand, smoothing the hair behind his ears, the nape of the neck. Finally, with his right thumb, he drew an oil cross over his forehead, his lips, and his heart. *May your will and your word be in my mind, on my lips, and in my heart.*

His left hand drew the blade up, lighting over his temple. The eyes shone with a radiance too great to extinguish, and he could see nothing else. He drew the blade back, feeling the first pull give way to soft grazing. His right hand guided it, pulling through the slick mass tight to his scalp in sharp, definite movements, the wet hunks of gold falling lifeless and sack-like onto the floor. All he knew now, were the eyes; nothing else could touch his mind, and the straightrazor worked in slow, thorough waves.

⊹

"What the hell have you done?"

"It's called Tonsure, Mother. It's a form of devotion."

"You look like a bedpost. Honest to God. Leonard! Get in here right now and see what your son has done now!"

Tommy sighed quietly and waited it out. They would never understand.

"Leonard!"

"I'm here! I'm here. What's all the—" He stopped halfway cross the kitchen floor and dropped the paintcan he'd been holding. All three fell silent.

⊹

His secret oratory had grown. An old lithograph of the Sacred Heart hung on one wall. Rosaries appeared in all sizes, with beads of various make-up. One from Fatima was strung with beads of crushed rose petal; another simply of enormous black glass beads, one of gold, one of pearl. Roses were brought here and died, their colorless husks becoming softly buried under the unseen fall of dust. The altar was covered with a silk now, of intricate Celtic design, looping rings and bold crosses. Beneath the silk was a pile of books and paraphernalia, from anthologies of the saints to cyclopedias to missiles to holy cards to the tiny silver points ending thin strips of thong.

⊹

"He won't eat, Leonard. I gave him his favorite, and he still won't eat. I don't know if he's angry at me, or what." The door was closed, on their bedroom, but light shone under the crack of the door.

"He'll come around when he gets hungry enough."

"Do you know how much you frustrate me? You don't seem to have any hold on the situation here. He's sick, Leonard. There's something wrong with him. And you don't see it."

"Maybe a little shy. I was too."

"Shy? That's not shy; it's sullen. And wherever he came from tonight, he was worse. Depressed. I could tell."

"Look, what do you want me to do?"

The light shifted with a movement in the room.

"Help me, with him, for Christ's sake. Just, do, something. I don't know. If I knew what to do, I'd do it myself." Her voice cracked and fell silent.

Across the hall, the Tommy's bedroom door closed with a slam.

Psychiatrist Log

He was positively the strangest case I've ever had. The temptation is to label him "schizophrenic with significant masochistic tendencies," and while this is a viable description, it's not complete. To say such would be too easy, a brushing simplification. Let me say first that I have no religious beliefs. Science eliminates the need for mythology, and even the science of the mind, which I am devoted to, helps to strip the foibles of these elaborate fantastic belief systems, namely by pinpointing the need for them and the process of building them, both on individual and collective levels. In swift summary, religion is the immediate practicality which eventually becomes the most obtuse impracticality. That which may have provided instant gratification for seekers of comfort, purpose, justification, discipline, superiority, an Eros relationship, or hope, in the end proves itself at least an impediment to growth (e.g. the freedom to question; involve naturally with others) and at most, renders its subscribers unable to function successfully in their world at large, and leads them to self-abasement, injury, and in extreme cases, death.

There you have it, the essence of my views, which I hold as fact, without formal presentation or defense required to suit them properly as a viable argument. Argument? I haven't any time nor desire for argument anymore. Let those who think differently do so. It matters not a whit to me. Unless, of course, such a one seeks my help. Then, only and always then, it is my duty to apply myself completely and to the best of my ability. If arguing theology against psychology is in order, then so be it.

He'd been sent to me because he had burned his hands. He was by no means the first masochistic child I had ever worked with, so I was not initially impressed nor intimidated by this one.

Tom was enrolled in St. Benedict's School for Boys, and became a regular altar boy almost immediately. St. Jude Church, School for the Enlightened transferred his academic records; nothing amiss there, high intelligence test profile, no discipline problems. His parents had forwarded his psychiatric papers to the school. I read them and the Mother Superior (the school principal) read them. They were brief and without description. Thomas Peterson had delusions translating into his Catholic religious belief system and was prone to masochism. Although he never made a sound about such things, it wasn't long before "things" started to manifest themselves. Generally they didn't attract much attention; Tom seemed a daydreamer, was all, but an excellent student so that was accepted. His biggest opposition was to be found not among his peers, but unfortunately in the halls of authority. Mother Superior, effectually the chief overseer and chaperone of the boys, took a disposition with Tom the moment he walked in. She had no tolerance for those considered special in any way or for daydreamers, let alone those whose minds seemed to wander when she was speaking. Ah well, we were bound to clash on the grounds of Tommy.

I kept a close eye to see whether the other boys had caught on to anything unusual in the new boy and singled him out for it, as boys are prone to do, but there is only so much that an adult can see, and he would never be bothered enough with such immediate matters to bring it up in confession. He seemed to be getting along inconspicuously enough. Since the veil of confession had never been raised between us, all of our conversations of significance began and ended in the box. He had to know that it was me to whom he spoke, if he took any notice at all. I longed to talk to him with more frequency than this, and thusly initiated the private confessions program for the school. As I suspected, with few exceptions, he was the only one to take advantage of the service, and so it did not interfere with my schedule much.

I liked to watch him at Mass. He was at every daily Mass, every one. He spoke to no one, but if someone were to speak to him, he would find the boy was a glow of happiness. What went through that mind during the Mass? So fervent was his expression, so unpretentious his oblivion, so unbroken his stare, that he was a moving sight to behold. As he received communion, and I noticed that he always made it a point to go to a priest rather than a lay distributor, his eyes seemed transfixed. I knew, through knowing him, that it would have been impossible to speak to him in such moments, and my own heart surged with a kind of thrill as I watched him cross back to his pew, in his daze. Then his eyes closed, and he was frozen on the kneeler, remaining long after the congregation had been seated, heard the announcements for baptisms and bingo, and in fact filed out. I never dreamt of disturbing him, and thusly he remained, after the Mass had ended, the holy vessels had been replaced into the tabernacle, the servers gone, the candles extinguished. Times I had gone back into the church in midafternoon and found him there yet, in the same fixed position, eyes closed.

Tape Number 23: Case 34A

Property of Minnesota Psychiatric Dept.
(Thomas Peterson and Dr. John M. Haines)

HAINES: "But perhaps God does not want you to suffer. Perhaps you would better serve him were you appreciative of the joy in the world, and the prospect of the world to come, and therefore in your state of happiness, you could pass more on."

PETERSON: "I do not object to happiness in itself. The ecstasies I feel when the Lord visits me are so acute that I pray that I would die in such moments, so exquisite is the bliss. No, I do not object to joy, but it is a rare thing, a privilege, granted by our Lord.

Beyond that, look around. The world is a tragic place, disappointing to Him times and times over. Humans do wrong. They do wrong to one another, they do wrong to themselves, they do wrong to the earth, and they do wrong to all. Nothing has been left untouched by man's blundering hands. Nothing is virgin.

Because there is so much sin and because the Devil is always at work, humans are always suffering. This grieves Him also. He does not wish to see men in pain."

HAINES: "You say this and yet, if He is omnipotent, He could end all suffering in the blink of an eye."

PETERSON: "You are so simple. He has many reasons for allowing humans to suffer, and we cannot know that it would not be worse, were He not merciful and granting alleviation all the time. Some must suffer for their sins. Wretched as their state may look to us, we cannot know the blackness of another's soul. Some suffer for others' sins, so that they may be forgiven. Some are merely victims of the Devil."

HAINES: "But again, if God is omnipotent, why is the Devil allowed reign at all? Indeed, why does he exist?"

PETERSON: "Man is sinful by nature. Justice must be done."

HAINES: "Why is man sinful by nature if God made his nature?"

PETERSON: "Because he sinned in the Garden. Woman introduced temptation,-"

HAINES: "So woman is more evil than man, the cause of his downfall?"

PETERSON: "The account is as it stands. They ate of the forbidden fruit. This is original sin."

HAINES: "Is this not absolved in baptism?"

PETERSON: "Yes, it is. But that does not cleanse the stain on man's soul. He is forever given to such shortcomings now."

HAINES: "What gives such precedence to the shortcoming of these two people in, presumably, the dawn of the world, neverminding that their existence is in direct opposition to all scientific truths about the creation of the world, proven beyond a reasonable doubt. If these two existed first and they committed this grievous sin, why has it left such a mark on the rest of humanity?"

PETERSON: "It showed the nature of man."

HAINES: "Whom God created—"

PETERSON: "It aroused His wrath."

HAINES: "Who is all-merciful—"

PETERSON: "And we can never know the ways of the Lord. He is so apart from our base humanity nature, that were we shown his true nature, we would still not understand."

HAINES: "I see. Well, then, we're out of luck."

End Tape

"Forgive me, Father, for I have sinned."

"What are your sins?"

"Pride."

"It is all right, my son. God sees all and understands. What you tell me, he already knows."

"But Father, I failed. He told me that He loves me. He told me that although I am base like the ground that I walk on, I am in his breast. I was told this because I should have seen the responsibilities it entailed, not to blind myself with arrogance. He was crying, Father, he was crying."

"Why was he crying?"

"He was crying because the world is such a lonely and desolate place for him, and he fears that were He to walk on earth again, there would be no one to take Him in. I told him all that I had done wrong in the day, and He cried more, Father. He cried again because my sins hurt Him worse, because I should know better, and yet I still sinned. I am afraid that I will sin again, Father. I am afraid that I will sin when I walk out of here, and that the thoughts will come, and I won't be able to stop them. Then what do I do?"

"Concentrate on the Lord and His mysteries, and you will not sin. That is what we all must do in times of temptation. In the name of the Lord Jesus, I absolve you of your sins. Go now and sin no more."

As the door closed behind the boy, I crossed myself. This, the greatest of his sins? Pride? Would that this were my greatest shortcoming. At least pride is the presence of something. Apathy is a void.

✛

At midnight a scream shot through the dormitory hall of St. Benedict's School for Boys. It was followed by another, and another, the terrified, uncontrolled screams of a wild animal. Lights flared on and doors flew open, dispatching the Mother Superior, three of her chaperone nuns, a janitor, and several scattered boys to the door of Tom's room. The Mother broke through immediately to his bedside. Tom was thrashing in all directions, the panicked sounds rushing in between stolen gasps.

"Tom Peterson! Wake up! Wake up!" He flayed at her, catching her sharply on the face. "Get over here! Pin him down!"

The oldest of the boys and the janitor tried to obey her. His limbs flew at such speed and with such strength that it took eight able-bodied people to gain some control over him, weighing down his arms, legs, middle, and head, for were one to be left to move, it would. At last, he was spread out on the bed. In a few moments, the ruthless screams subdued into a breathless kind of grunting, and his eyes shut.

"Tom? Tom?" Hands on his head, she looked closely into his face. "Tom?"

Nothing. No response.

One of the nuns spoke up. "Should I call a doctor?"

"A doctor? No. He's had a bad dream, that's all."

"He's not epileptic or . . ."

"He's fine, sister." Her voice rose sharply. "There is nothing wrong here, other than Tom had a bad dream. Now all of you boys go back to bed and turn out your lights immediately. Show's over. I want to hear no sound tonight coming from your rooms. Go."

Those who had helped relinquished their holds on the young frame and took a parting scan over the whole picture, to talk about later. The janitor wavered for a moment, staring at Tom, then at the Mother.

"Thanks, George. You may go back to work now."

The door closed behind him. The nuns began to breathe a little easier, and looked to one another. The Mother began rearranging the blankets over him. They had settled themselves and were about to leave for their wing, when the door opened again. I was cursing the distance between the rectory and the school.

"Hello. Sorry I took so long to get here."

"That's fine, Father. Everything's under control here, and Mr. Peterson has gone back to sleep."

I crossed to the bed and looked closely at Tom's face, still flushed and disheveled. "Did he wake? I mean, did he speak at all?"

"Just yelled a lot. Nightmare."

"So I hear." She peered at me, as if she would be able to detect something if she just looked hard enough.

"Well, Father, looks like that's it for tonight. We all may as well go back to bed."

"Thanks. Well, you go on ahead."

She seemed caught for a moment, waiting for me, her brows drawing together sharply, then one of the nuns caught her eye. She turned to her. "All right, let's go."

I sat up with him for the better part of an hour. His face was still taut, and now and then a film of moisture appeared on his forehead. He remained still, lying on his back. Without warning, his head turned and his eyes opened, directly on me. I tried to look kind.

"Hello, Tom. It's Father."

"Is it time for confession?"

"It can be, if you like. Do you want me to hear your confession?"

He nodded, eyes unnaturally wide. I blessed the room, made the sign of the cross, and opened the confession. His voice was tired but full of purpose.

"I am afraid of going to hell."

"It is a scary idea. Do you think that you will?"

He blinked, gathering his thoughts. "I could. The Devil was here tonight, and he said that he wants my soul; he's going to lure me away; he showed me how I would look if I were full of evil." This caught him, and for the first time, I was able to see the changes in his expression during these moments of silence. For such a private boy, his face was blatantly public, and betrayed each thread of his struggle. I wondered suddenly how he would look when lost in one of his raptures. He was truly disturbed by the thought in him now.

"How did you look when you were evil?"

The skin over his eyes pulled tightly. "My eyes . . . were red. All red, not bright red, but a red like blood, and my face was all dark, just dark, just very . . . " He broke off, eyes still closed.

"What else did you see? Anything?" I was hoping to hear that he'd seen Christ, not for my sake, but because it would relieve him of this enormous strain. He took a moment, and then opened his eyes on me again. In a voice hushed with astonishment and horror, he said, "I saw hell."

"Hell? What did it look like?"

"It wasn't all fire like the pictures. It was black, almost all black. I almost couldn't see anything, except that he shined his eyes, and revealed all souls hanging, unable to move, they were frozen and limp, in little chambers, like small caves, but not rock at all. And the souls were the horrible thing, Father. They were the horrible thing. They were shadows with shoulders and heads, but not much else, and they gave off a great stench so that I couldn't breathe, and as I got closer, I was afraid to look at their faces, what their eyes would look like, and their mouths, and would they be rotting or tortured, or forever trapped in the pain of death, with terrified, frozen screams caught in tongues of fire. I tried to run from seeing them, from having to face them, and he shoved me so close to one that I couldn't breathe from the smell, and he pulled my eyelids back, and I saw . . . that the soul . . . didn't have any face at all, no eyes, no nothing, it was blank, and this was, Father, so unimaginably horrid that I screamed, I screamed so loudly that my ears shrank in shock, and he let me go . . . he let me go . . ."

The air seemed to go out of him, and he sank into the bed like a wet blanket. His eyes slid shut and his breathing came very heavily. I knew he would sleep now, and put my hand on his wet forehead, which was now very cold, and blessed him. He didn't move, and his breathing stayed deeply constant. I finished my prayers and went back to the rectory, the night clear and cool.

✠

"Father, I couldn't help but hearing what went on last night. Wonder if you think it was just a nightmare, after all?"

Nothing escaped Hilda. Nothing. I worked on finishing my lunch. "Well, what do you think?"

She sat down and arranged to eat her own sandwich. "If you ask me, Father, a bad dream doesn't act like that. I've had four boys, and I know a bad dream when I see one."

"But you didn't see Tom."

"No, but I heard all about it. Really sounds to me like he might need to see someone."

"A doctor?"

"Maybe, yes."

I set down my glass. "Why is it that a boy can't just have a bad night around here? He doesn't need a doctor. If I think he does, then I won't hesitate to send him one. Or to let his parents send him to one."

She refilled my glass and said in a soothing voice, "His parents know what went on. Mother Superior called them this morning."

I stared at her. Of course, it was within her province to call. Still, it burned in my stomach to think that she had.

"They didn't seem surprised, and gave permission for whatever treatment we thought necessary."

"I see. And has she decided what we think necessary?" This was catty, and I should watch myself, I thought.

"Not really. Some mild sedatives for a while."

I knew I was finished eating. I forced myself to look at the newspaper for a very long three minutes, and rose.

"Well, thanks for a good lunch. I'd better get started on the afternoon."

"Salmon tonight; don't be late."

"Great."

☩

It was a heated discussion, and I won't go into the details, but in the end, Mother shelved the idea of sleeping pills, at least for a while.

Tape Number 27: Case 34A

Property of Minnesota Psychiatry Department

HAINES: "And you think that a merciful God would allow you to know such horrors as these "dark visions" and disrupt everyone around you with them?"

PETERSON: "God works through His children, using them as vessels. If you haven't been to a city, and you need directions on how to get there, isn't it better to talk to someone who had been there?"

HAINES: "I wouldn't need you to go there, if it was out of your way, just to give me directions. I can follow directions from a map."

PETERSON: "But with a guide, you know just what it is you are going to."

HAINES: "I must already have an idea if I want to go there in the first place. And I know that the city exists whether you've been there or not."

PETERSON: "All right, so what you're saying, is that it is an independent journey. It is. The journey of faith is something no one need witness but Christ. But it may help someone, somewhere along the way, to have assurance that they are going the right way."

HAINES: "But a person giving the help can only give their highest help if it is of their own free will to do so. If you see yourself as this assistant, this direction beacon, then why is it that you have no choice in the matter?"

PETERSON: "God has chosen me. He has given me this duty."

HAINES: "And if you did not want it?"

PETERSON: "I want nothing outside of the Lord's will."

HAINES: "You are a free and complete organism, unto

yourself, as all people are."

PETERSON: "I am not complete without God, and my freedom is within the perimeters of His Will."

HAINES: "Is it not possible that you, yourself, could want something different for yourself than what God wants for you?"

PETERSON: "Possible, yes. But that is often the Devil's influence."

HAINES: "Must your desires be only of God or of the Devil? Can't you have any originate within yourself?"

PETERSON: "Yes, they do. Of course."

HAINES: "And if they are contrary to God's wishes?"

PETERSON: "Then I must overlook my selfish, narrow vision, because I cannot know all that He knows; He knows what is best."

HAINES: "Have you no free will?"

PETERSON: "My will is determined by God."

HAINES: "And if God tells you to stop eating?"

PETERSON: "I do."

HAINES: "When do you start again?"

PETERSON: "When He says that I may."

HAINES: "What if He tells you a week from now?"

PETERSON: "I restart a week from now."

HAINES: "What if he tells you a month from now?"

PETERSON: "I restart a month from now."

HAINES: "Two months? Three months?"

PETERSON: "If the Lord told me to start in five years, I would touch no food for five years."

HAINES: "So you destroy the very organism, the miraculous work of art, as you yourself have called it, that He created?"

PETERSON: "If He wills it. St. Theresa Neumann didn't eat or drink or sleep for many years under His orders. In fact, she wanted to but could not."

HAINES: "Several years? Why would a loving god subject anyone to such a thing?"

PETERSON: "We cannot know why he would will such a thing. We cannot understand the reasoning of God."

HAINES: "But don't you wonder?! Haven't you the slightest questioning about it? It is a logical, natural questioning. To accept without question is to deliberately stint the powers of thinking."

PETERSON: "It is to have faith."

HAINES: "Faith, then, would have us accept all suffering without question. Faith would have us ignore any questioning of the morality and process of disease and injury. Faith doesn't need minds. It needs an emptying of minds, and blind, marionette obedience. If we all had faith, there would be no hospitals. There would be no medical field. No schools, no books, no discussions, no questions. Ignorance would be king."

PETERSON: "Christ would be king. To have faith is to empty oneself of self, and only obey God's commands without question."

HAINES: "Then you may die. And every person afflicted in any way may die because there can be no investigation into alternatives."

PETERSON: "That may be. God's will would prevail. Miracles happen, like St. Theresa being able to survive without eating or drinking for many years."

HAINES: "What makes you so sure that story is true?"

[pause]

PETERSON: "True? Of course it's true. It's true."

HAINES: "How do you know?"

PETERSON: "I know because I have faith. The person who wrote the account also had faith as did St. Theresa."

HAINES: "So you all have faith?"

PETERSON: "Yes."

HAINES: "And through faith you know that it is true?"

PETERSON: "Yes."

HAINES: "I have here another book, certainly not the only one of its perspective, which claims that Theresa was a good person, titled a saint, but that the story concerning her abstinence is false, that such deprivation would be impossible."

PETERSON: "It is not a book written by one who has faith."

HAINES: "It is written by a member of a holy order, and acknowledged by all within it."

PETERSON: "The story is true."

HAINES: "He says that St. George, protector of England, can be no more than a legend; he purportedly slew a dragon! St. Barlaam and St. Josaphat never existed. They were adopted from the Indian story of Siddhartha Buddha. The martyr St. Barbara, whose father shut her away in a tower because of her unfailing beauty, has been honored from 235 in Egypt. Today she is honored as the patron saint of gunners and miners. And yet there is no evidence whatsoever that she ever existed.

"Of course the tale of the very famous St. Katherine of Alexandria is preposterous. She was imprisoned, fed by a dove, and stretched out on a spiked wheel, which killed several onlookers in its subsequent explosion. When she was killed, by beheading, milk, not blood, flowed out. St. Pantaleon, or Panteleimon, could not be killed either: they tried burning, liquid lead, drowning, wild beasts, the wheel, and the sword. Finally he was killed by beheading, again with the flow of milk, and the Olive tree he was bound to suddenly sprang into fruit.

"Of St. Christina the Astonishing, the Lives of the Saints

states that "Allowances must be made for exaggeration, misunderstanding, and the desire to be edifying according to the mind of the writer and his time; but even when this has been done, there is little in the recorded history of Christina of Brusthem to make us think she was other than a pathological case." (176)

"St. Margaret, also called Marina, was swallowed by the devil who assumed the form of a dragon, but the cross she was holding irritated his stomach until he spat her out."

PETERSON: "And so I spit on your heresy and sacriledge. If you'll excuse me, I must be going."

End Tape

ometime during Advent, he was serving Mass for a guest priest. I wasn't there, but I heard all about it. "Take a deep breath."

The congregation was more silent than they had been the entire Mass.

"Relax. Can you stand? Don't rush it."

Lector Dr. Richards had stepped in immediately, when he saw Tom's face fall pale as his server robe. The Mass had been approaching the point of transubstantiation:

"We most humbly beseech Thee, almighty God; command these offerings to be borne by the hands of Thy holy Angels to Thine altar on high, in the sight of Thy divine majesty, that as many as shall partake of the most holy Body and Blood of Thy Son at this altar."

Tom's stare was broken by a flickering of his eyelids.

"Behold the Lamb of God, behold Him who takest away the sins of the world. Blessed are those who are called to the Lamb's supper."

The priest's hands raised the white circular host high over his downcast head. Tom wavered and went down with a slump. Dr. Richard's quick interception saved the boy's head from impacting the marble floor. Now Tommy was on his feet, being led into the sacristy.

"Just sit and take a deep breath. Easy does it."

He was staring straight ahead, past the doctor, as if something were commanding his attention. His robe had been taken off and the man was speaking to him.

"So what happened out there?"

The black cloak of Mother Superior separated the two with a wrench.

"I'll tell you what happened out there. Our center stage altar boy wanted the world to know he was having one of his visions. Isn't that right, Mr. Peterson?"

His stare went on unbroken.

"Don't pull that on me. I know very well you hear me when I'm talking to you. I said you wanted the world to know that the Lord was making one of his alleged personal visitations to you, the great saint of our day and time. Well, I'll tell you, it may work with them, and it may work with your corrupted family, but it doesn't work with me. Understand? Do you understand? I said, do you understand?!"

She wrenched him toward her with a grab round his belt. She cried out and looked at her hand. It was bleeding. She looked at him, her mouth wide, and grabbed his jeans again. She undid his belt and zipper and yanked down the waist of his jeans, displaying a rim of silver studs and pink, raw flesh.

✠

"That boy is a saint, Sister."

"He has more evil in him than all of us combined. You just can't see it. You should watch this boy closely."

"I watch him all the time, Sister. I watch him when he eats, I watch him when he prays, and I watch him when he sleeps. I hear his confessions!"

"He afflicts himself, Father. The waistline of his jeans is lined with spurs! Tell me that you condone such behavior."

"I am not at liberty to discuss his reasons for doing such

things. Suffice it to say that such acts have shaped many a soul in the history of the church and are rarely understood by lay people."

"How dare you. I am not a lay person, but a servant of the Lord. How -"

"Any people. All people. St. Simeon Stylites continually wore a girdle of pointed wire and ate nothing for the entire forty days of Lent. St. Theresa lowered her lips to a bedpan in an act of humility, because she was empty of any false pride."

"That was different."

"Why? Our own Lord endured the greatest suffering possible. This Faith is not afraid of suffering! We fast. We do penance for our sins. We suffer for them now so that in the next world, we will not have to. "Suffer, little children to come to me." "

"It's not the same thing."

"Why not? Because these were people whom you did not know? You can accept it in a written story, and pray with it in mind, but cannot see it before your very eyes? What does he have to do, what does he have to be, for you to believe in his suffering as valid? Where is the proof that he is anything, anything, other than true sainthood, in our midst?"

"A saint, to me, would be somehow recognizable. In a saint's company, I would feel the purity there, the kindness, the otherworldliness. This boy has no such effect. He is withdrawn, curt, and gives the appearance that he is better than those around him. He is full of pride, and unnecessarily so. Furthermore, the boy has no humor."

"Sister, I think what you have is a personal dislike for the boy. He has done nothing wrong. On the contrary, he is a model church servant in every way, fulfilling all his duties, spending late hours kneeling at the rail, saying daily rosaries, giving impeccable obedience to his superiors. Simply because he does not bring you cigarettes and tell you jokes or have a floating halo is no reason to judge him. Look at his actions. Moreover, why don't you look to your own. And I'll look to mine, and we'll all be happy. Good day, Sister."

Minnesota

School for the Enlightened, elementary division

The priest stood before the room of children and adjusted his podium. A glass of water had been placed on a nearby table, and the desks were arranged arena-fashion around him. He finally stopped fidgeting and looked over the classroom. Thoroughly attentive elementary schoolers, from various grades. Tom fixed on him with quiet eyes. He cleared his throat.

"How many of you know the story of the Passion and the Crucifixion?"

Each child raised a hand.

"Yes, we've all heard it, but today I want to really talk about it, for a while. Now, Christ's sufferings didn't begin when the soldiers came and took him away. The pain that He felt in fearing his doom was praying on him for some time, especially the night before. You may have heard that he sweat blood. This was not a simple sweating that happened to be tinged with pink. There is a medical condition wherein the body is under such duress that the heart beats with unimaginable speed. The capillaries become engorged with the frenzied hyperactive coursing of blood, swelling with the unbearable pressure of the current, until the blood is moving at too great a pace to be managed by the body, and it forces through the walls of the capillaries, tears through the three layers of skin, and squeezes out the tiny pores. This condition is exceedingly rare, and only ninety percent of those who experience it do not even survive. He remained thus for some hours, until he was abducted by the Roman officials and thrown into a cell for the night.

There was no sleep for him in this cell, only abuse in rounds of prison wardens, who, instead of protecting the prisoners, considered them completely at their mercy, and beat Christ freely throughout the night. He was kicked, punched, sworn at and spit on by armed strangers against whom he had no defense.

Once he was brought before the people and judged guilty

of blasphemy, a crown of long and sharp thorns was forced onto his head, with such force that it was actually imbedded. The Shroud of Turin shows that one thorn stuck straight into his right eye.

He was whipped. The process of whipping at the time consisted of three stages, meaning three whips. The first whip was constructed of thin strips of leather tipped with pieces of bone and stone, designed to clot the blood at the surface. The second was a simple leather whip, which burst the blood blisters under the skin. The third had tiny metal hooks on the ends of leather strips. These hooked into the skin and tore it up, searing openings for the mottled blood bruises to run out of. But now he was so covered in blood and raw flesh that he was barely recognizable as a human being. He was one large heap of bloodied meat that could barely move."

One child raised his hand and fled for the bathroom. A splattering sound on the hallway floor told that she hadn't made it.

The cross itself was not of a small letter T shape, as is often depicted in art and things claiming to be art, but rather one beam was settled across another with notches, creating a shape like a capital T. The horizontal beam typically weighed about two hundred pounds, and it was strapped across shoulders for him to carry, staggering and falling, up to Mount Calvary. And all the way up the hill he was at the mercy of the huge crowd, most of whom turned out regularly for these crucifixions, to be entertained.

Now consider the depictions of crucifixions that you have seen. Most show Christ with a spot of blood on either palm. Wrong. The nails would simply have stripped out between the fingers. There is a small hollow just below the hand, in the wrist, that can support the body's weight under crucifixion. Most of the criminals were only tied to their crosses. Christ had a spike driven through this space, bending and splitting the bones in the wrist, severing the nerves and snapping the veins apart."

A mesmerized boy spoke without raising his hand.

"But isn't that where people slit their wrists to die? Wouldn't he be dead by now?"

"The nails in the feet were driven right through the middle of them. When the body was raised, the effect on the posture was such that the head was pulled down into the chest, driving the chin into the ribs, threatening asphyxiation. And asphyxiation this way was how the prisoners usually died. In the meantime, they pushed themselves continually upwards to raise the head for breath, driving the feet against the nails, and arching the back dramatically. This put great stress on the arms, radiating from the nails there.

So when the soldiers came to break the legs, this was not out of cruelty, but of final release, preventing the victim from pushing himself up any more, and so he would die, unable to get air. Christ, however, was already dead when they got to him. Little wonder. Still, one soldier plunged a spear into his side to be sure, and blood and water flowed out.

It is His suffering that we must keep alive in our hearts and our heads every moment of every day, and never forget, for none of us could ever suffer so much. In truth, we actually could not. After the sweating of the blood, it simply would not be possible for a human being to survive any fraction of these trials. There can never be enough compensation for the Lord's suffering, and it was for you, for all that you do wrong. Look hard at that next piece of candy which you don't really need and then look, twice as hard, at the crucifix, and think whether you really have a right to such excess. You may be a child, but that is in no way an excuse for any small sin that you commit. Remember the bloody face of our Lord."

He took a drink of the water. A female teacher approached him.

"Thank you so much, Father. That was just beautiful. Don't miss our bake sale on the way out.

Minnesota

He sat in the semi-darkness of his oratory, waiting for the night sky to close the room off completely from the world. He loved the tall candles, the swirling sides that oozed the wax down the sides like blood from the Holy Wounds. What could he do, he thought, what could he say, to make his family understand? They were good hearted, he knew, but they would never be truly good. He removed the calendar stick from beneath the altar, making another notch on the gathering line of notches for the days. His mother would never understand what it was to fast; she simply would never know. The statue looked at him with eyes of reserve, the eternal flow of love held carefully in waiting, like one almost asleep. *Wake Me,* it said. *Pour out your life for me, and empty yourself of that which you do not need. Gluttony is a sin, and there are those of My loved ones who will benefit from your sacrifice.* The boy closed his eyes, swooning in blissful numbness. Yes, he would do as his Lord required. He would gladly lay down his life, if asked. With a hard stare at the Sacred Heart, he walked round the back of the shack, knelt, crossed himself, closed his eyes and breathed deep. He saw them, the starving, the masses of the hungry, almost not human with their shrunken, clinging skin, their protruding bones. Large, insupportable heads with wide eyes, distended abdomens swelling from imploding grief, they were sticks, and elbows, racked angles swarmed over with flies, this nebulous of Devil's victims, powerless and never more in need of help. He held out his hands, tragically human, and then saw the white hands of Christ, the perfect, smooth, and pure, defaced with the horrible reminders pitting beneath the palms. The whiteness intensified to a blaze, blinding him, scalding his own hands. He forced the fingers to work and pulled his arm in, extending his index finger through the searing touch of the divine light, and put it deep into his throat, the heat rising to his nose and his eyes. It came pouring out, the horror, the gluttony, the unsightly sin of luxury and indulgence. His breath fought to grab through the upheaval, but he only thrusted harder, his throat beating red and Christ's hands beginning to bleed. Sometime through the blood the light turned to darkness, and the world stood silent again, beginning its crickets and the quiet sounds of night. He head was bent over his knees, and the vision was gone. *I offer this for the starving, and the forgiveness of us sinners.* "You will always have the poor," Jesus said.

Tape Number 32: Case 34A

Property of Minnesota Psychiatry Dept.

HAINES: "Is it possible to have faith without pain?"

PETERSON: "No. Pain is inevitable on many levels; first, the initial embrace of the faith involves a dying of the former self, renunciation of old beliefs, adjustment to new, or simply the sudden fill of what was before a void. The introduction is the first rocky launch into a foreign land. For not only must you accept the faith; the faith must accept you.

"Secondly, faith involves constant striving toward perfection, which necessitates constant change. Since man can never be perfect, this pursuit goes on throughout his entire life, bringing change, and change is painful.

"As this personal faith between God and man develops, man is drawn farther and farther into God and the unseen realm, consequently leaving this world farther behind. While the man's ultimate joy and destiny is to be completely absorbed into that world and to leave this one behind, as these roots become severed, he will feel the alienation and the loss of what he held dear here: family, loved ones, possessions, perhaps menial activities that pleased the body, from sports to sexual involvement to immoderate and excessive eating habits."

HAINES: "These things are all left behind? That which brought the man joy before?"

PETERSON: "On most paths, no. Most humans cannot sacrifice such indulgences, and so never reach the level of sanctity which we are discussing. But the truly holy, those who are focused and disciplined, shed these worthless distractions."

HAINES: "But these are the very things which make us human, which we enjoy specifically as humans. This is what sets us apart."

PETERSON: "Of course not. Your thinking is flawed at very basic and ingrained levels here. This is a flaw in human nature comprising its incorrigible arrogance. Man is certainly above the animals. *These things are here for you to enjoy.*"

HAINES: "Do you not enjoy your teachers? Do you not enjoy learning? Learning, the power to reason, is the thing which to many sets humans apart. If so, than this sets humans apart in a way that is below the animals, as students at their feet."

PETERSON: "The joy of learning can only be fulfilled at its highest level, from the ultimate teacher Himself. But it is not this not what separates humans in the eyes of the Church. It is simply the possession of a soul. Man alone possesses a soul; no other creature does."

HAINES: "And so all men are above any other creature by this virtue alone? If the soul is something which sets a creature above, than it seems that a thoroughly logical god would have placed it as something to be obtained, not inherent. So is man superior by virtue of being man, or is it because he attains the goodness you desire?"

PETERSON: "His original superiority carries regardless of what he does. He can, through severe evil, reduce himself to a state below the animals, but the retention of his status dictates that now his penance and punishment will be greater than would an animal's, in proportion to his superiority. Man is superior to other creatures in the sense of his station in this world, but he often does not live up to what is expected of him (in this station), which is what would set him not only superior to beast in station, but also in virtue."

HAINES: "Your point, in summary, is that man is by nature above all others, though he can disgrace himself herein."

PETERSON: "Yes."

HAINES: "I wonder whether you have spent any time outdoors."

PETERSON: "What?"

HAINES: "To the point, though, of physical activity, and examples you mentioned, you mean anything physical, be it primary need, such as eating, or secondary, say sport. You mean to say that a natural path of holiness will preclude these instinctively natural urges?"

PETERSON: "A pure path has no room for deflections of thought, like a game which not only wastes valuable time on this planet which could otherwise have been spent is servitude, but encourages vanity in competition, physical appearance, and the mastery of a wholly unimportant and otherwise useless skill. And as for saying that these practices, especially sexual involvement, are what set humans apart, that is a completely ludicrous, and gravely wrong statement. These things are no further above the ground than the rat which also engages in them. They are base impulses which are to be realized and overcome, risen above, in the pursuit of a higher state of being."

HAINES: "You will agree that it occurs to all men, of all cultures, throughout all of time, to have such impulses as sexual and playful, while the "natural path" of the seldom obtained, and therefore unnatural state, of holiness occurs to only a few?"

PETERSON: "Certainly. The Devil is everywhere. Temptation is everywhere. Many are called, but few are chosen."

HAINES: "It doesn't seem to me, though, that many *are* called, if the path to sainthood is what you mean that they are called to. How would a small tribe in a corner of the tropics ever know that they should desire to achieve sainthood, let alone how to go about doing it? I quote to you from *The Eagle and the Dove**: 'In other words, is it or is it not conceivable

---

* *The Eagle and the Dove*, V. Sackville-West, page 36.

that in the hypothetical case of a person who had never heard of God, Christ, the Communion of Saints, the Devil, or any of the accepted appurtenances of religion, the phenomenon of divine visions or locutions should occur? ... Is it possible to imagine a stigmatist to whom the story of the Crucifixion should be totally unknown? Is it possible to imagine our Lady appearing to one who was unacquainted with the story of Christ's nativity? If such cases exist, proven beyond suspicion, they would seem to settle the matter once and for all; but in their absence it would seem logical to conclude that the phenomena of mystical theology must take their origin from some image already in the mind.'

"What God is so feeble that he needs men to go into these regions and teach? Would it not be more sensible, peaceful, and easier, to simply create the natural state of his creatures be the natural state of holiness? Man is far outnumbered by other creatures, the ones without souls. Wouldn't it be better to have the commonalties within all of these natures be complimentary to one another, and ultimately to the higher path that He wishes to instill in all? Wouldn't it be more sensible to have the things which he would have man finally rise to be evident and apparent all around him, rather than something which is completely foreign to one ignorant of the faith and something completely contrary to the basic nature of man? What sense is it that humans must spend their entire lifetimes on this earth living contrary to their natural impulses, in opposition to all they see around them operating on a natural level, try to disengage themselves from the world and the being in which they are, to a world which is not the one into which they have been born, and in which they will most certainly die? It is only man who is in such states of unhappiness and struggle with his "place in the universe." The animals, if left to their own accord, function in a balanced and symbiotic system."

PETERSON: "A system created by God."

HAINES: "But nevermind the sense of it from man's point of view. Is it not is misuse of the tool which you hold that their creator gave them, that is, their body? And their world? Wouldn't it be more honorable to glory in the body, and love it, admire it and be appreciative of it, for it is perhaps their greatest gift from this creator, and presumably, he approves of it, even, to further your beliefs, dwells in it? What service can come of denying its very essence, abilities, pleasures, and those things which make it stronger?"

PETERSON: "You are lumping together too many things—food, sport, sexual activity! Surely you do not think that sexual intercourse serves the body in such ways."

HAINES: "Oh, but I do! I know that it does! Besides being medical fact, it is simply obvious. In the context of your faith, I would say to you this: that a body well-sexed is in better cardiovascular condition, which lays the basic stamina for a body. Such a body is conditioned muscularly, the bloodflow and metabolism increased and encouraged, cell growth enhanced, the nerves steadied, endorphins released, and the complexion flushed to clear. Now, such a body, and such is any body well-worked through any wholesome physical activity, is at its optimum potential to carry out any work that you would have it do. It is strong, resilient, obedient, and capable of more than the body which habitually lies dormant. What can you find wrong with that? Where is the advantage of a person lying sick and helpless, needing to be tended, who can do little other than survive?"

PETERSON: "You do not understand the beauty, nor the function, nor the rewards of suffering."

End Tape

The blue and red films falling on his skin through the stained glass windows gave a life to him, as if he were engulfed in fire. The sweat shined deeply under the colors, melting him beneath the flame. What was it that went on inside his head? Hours had passed. He hadn't moved once. The marble rail had to be hard against his knees. No one else was in the church, the sanctuary candle and the devotional votives being the only illumination besides effects of the bright moonlight through the windows.

I sat in a back pew, hands folded in my lap. He was an enigma, but a genuine one, silent in his extraordinariness. I hadn't ever mastered the art of being silent. My father had. His was a constant silence, but likely to be encasing a grudge of some sort. If nothing else, it would be a signal that he was deep into his latest bottle of whiskey, and shouldn't be disturbed. I knew the difference between a particular silence like that and his usual silent disposition. My mother had dealt with it well, so far as I could remember, persisting in her innocent, chatty cheerfulness, regardless of how much it irritated him. I had always been glad of that, when witnessing it, but held some breath in check on her account. She was playing with fire, after all, at such times.

His outline took up nearly the whole armchair, arms spreading out over the slipcovers my mother had carefully screwed down on this as well as all the furniture. His silhouette was far worse than the revealed man however. The standing metal lamp showed a swarthy mastodon, with unsmoothable furrows over his brows and around his pulled-down mouth. The hair was almost always grey, though, no matter how far back I looked into memory. As large as I was now, through my youth, I was only tall and thin, and somehow, however much taller you are than another, you are still the weaker one if you haven't the bulk. I always hated that fact.

I was looking down at him, with the paper in my hand. I was all of twenty-two; today that would have me in my own apartment paying water bills. Then it had me the boy under my father's roof.

"You did what?"

"I wrote to this seminary. They said they will accept me. The program starts in three months. It will take a long time, because I have to be recognized as a Catholic first."

His eyes, for all their vesselled redness, were as dark as a closet. "What do you mean, writing to some damn Catholic thing? To what?"

"To enter seminary. To become a priest."

His hand had been on the shoe tree by his chair. Suddenly it caught me in a sharp blindness on my right temple. I reeled and steadied myself against the coffee table.

"Stephan, what's going on in there?" Mother had been in the kitchen, and knew the sounds of disturbance. She had her apron on.

"This fool thinks he wants to be a Catholic priest."

She was so sweet, just so simple. I don't know if she even realized what Catholic was.

"Do you now? Oh, well, that's something."

"I've got the acceptance letter from seminary." My entire conversion had been going on surreptitiously. I'd been afraid to bring it up because of this, just this. "I would move, Mother, in three months."

"Move? Where to?"

"That's enough of this! I don't want to hear any more! Understand?"

My head was still swimming. Somehow, I got up the nerve to stand up to him. I don't know where it came from.

"I'm serious. This is what I want to do."

I had rarely seen him in a rage like this one. It was huge, larger than the two of us standing there looking at him in fear, and it exploded now, as he shot out of the chair. I still stood taller than him. He grabbed me by the shoulder and wrenched me toward him. My mother started to shout at him, and before I could understand what was happening, he had punched me twice on the jaw.

"You are not Catholic! We are not Catholic! I will have no Catholic son! If you call yourself one of them, I disown you. Hear? You will be dead to this house!" With that he grabbed the paper from seminary and tore it, straight down the middle and then three times in odd directions. He threw the mess up into the space between us. One piece landed in my hair. I was on the floor, and my mother was being a nuisance trying to nurse my injuries. She picked up the paper, not knowing, I suppose, what else to do, and my Father left the house with a slam of the screen door. My mother's purse lay dumped out through the kitchen doorway. Little wonder where he'd gone.

I stared at my hands. They were almost as large as I remembered his, now. In fact, they probably were as large as his, but the mind's eye wouldn't permit such an irony of proportion. My breath came in a long, slow draught, and my eyes drifted back up to the space where Tom had been praying. He was gone now. Oh, I'd missed him leave. I rose slowly and drifted up to the rail, staring at the window Tommy had been underneath. The Holy Mother looked down at me in blue-shrouded compassion, so thick it was like a voice, so thin and non-existant that a stone in the pane would shatter it forever. I looked down at the spot where Tommy had been. There was a thin trickle of blood across the step.

·✝·

It was the Holy Hour of Reparation. I stood in the aisle facing the congregation, with four altar servers behind me, two girls and two boys. Two held pillars of candles, one held the processional crucifix, lifting it nearly twelve feet into the air, and one carried the book before me so that I could read it without pausing in the heavy sway of the censure, pouring out curls of incense. The procession had led round the church. I was distracted by a child pulling one of her mother's huge earrings off in the lower scope of my peripheral vision. I found that I needed more focus, if I was to keep the pious expression of the Reverend Mother on my right from invading my thoughts. I raised my voice more, emphasizing words in the text, concentrating on the words on the page. We stopped before the sanctuary. I read:

"The Sacred Heart of Jesus began this devotion of the Holy Hour of Reparation when He entered the Garden of Gethsemani on Mount Olivet. He said to the Apostles, 'My soul is sorrowful even unto death. Stay you here and watch with me.' Later He said to them: 'Could you not watch one hour with me? Watch and pray, that you enter not into temptation.'"

This one really affected Tom. Besides the sweats, his face was drawn and appeared gaunt through the play of sudden paleness and shadow. I tried not to watch him, as I always tried; yet there he was, riveting my attention in between stares at the page.

"As Jesus spoke to His Apostles, so He pleads with us to stay and watch and pray with Him. His Sacred Heart is filled with sadness, because so many doubt Him, despise Him, insult Him, ridicule Him, spit upon Him, slap Him, accuse Him, condemn Him. In the Sacrament of His Love, so many forget Him. Every mortal sin brings down the terrible scourges on His Sacred Body, presses the sharp thorns into His Sacred Head, and hammers the cruel nails into His Sacred Hands and Feet. The ingratitude of mankind continually pierces His Sacred Heart.

The Sacred Heart of Jesus said to St. Margaret Mary: 'Make reparation for the ingratitude of men. Spend an hour in prayer to appease divine justice, to implore mercy for sinners, to honor Me, to console Me for My bitter suffering when abandoned by My Apostles, when they did not watch one hour with Me.'*

In the final stages, I stood beneath the crucifix, the altar servers on either side of me with thinner candles, and one by one, we prayed to the Holy Wounds. The eyes of the attentive shifted with each prayer, staring at the wound being venerated.

I led the prayer to the Wound of the Left Foot. As we recited the prayers to the wounds, his pallor began to change. It was as if life itself kissed him on the lips. The glow of pink began to rise and warm his skin, effusive in its excited entrance. I led the prayer to the Wound of the Right Foot. Tom reached the peak of the perfect healthful appearance, and he was a beauty to behold, youth restored and fresher than he had ever known. I led the prayer to the Wound of the Left Hand. It didn't stop. The color deepened, becoming a blush, the misty pink growing heavier and heavier. His face was red, plain and simple, the red becoming so sharp that anyone, were they to see him, would take notice. I led the prayer to the Wound of the Right Hand. The red was red beet red, and a wave of alarm passed through me at the altar. I couldn't see the eyes; the eyes were closed, but his color, and the fact that it was sustaining its deep shade, was a sign of something. Finally, I led the prayer to the Wound of the Sacred Side. Tom had far passed the

---

* *Soul Assurance Prayer Plan*, 1945

point of a reasonable flush, and I fought to keep my focus on conducting the Holy Hour. My voice increased in tempo, just subtly, but it did. After about fifteen more minutes, the ceremony ended.

Even on a solemn day of the church calendar, it is a labor to pull through the tangles of social hooks. They simply change form, shifting from the smothering effervescence of dinner invitations and homily praise and introductions, to subdued tones of stern importance, telling of hospitalizations, deaths, and memories. It was all so predictable. I wondered which came first—the occasion or the mood. I saw it through as efficiently as I could, took on a very few new obligations and appointments, and then they were all gone, all, that is, except the form of a thin young man with a cowlick sticking up. It was almost nine o'clock in the evening, and he was walking toward the side door. I picked up my step in the aisle.

"Tom, could I have a minute?"

"Of course, Father." I caught up to him, and quietly caught my breath up with me.

"How do you feel?"

"Fine, thanks."

"I'm kind of concerned, actually. Your face is extremely red. Do you have a fever?"

His eyes glazed over for a moment, partly with that great kindness, and partly his usual removal. I waited for him to come back. "I don't know."

"Let's have you come over to the rectory for a moment or two. Hilda's there, and we'll let her have a quick look at you."

✠

Hilda had been steeping a pot of tea to greet me. I didn't need to say anything. No sooner were we in the door, than her hands were on Tom's face.

"Good Night! This boy has a fever that could cook eggs. Sit down with Father while I find the thermometer."

We sat next to one another at the little round kitchen table. She was gone only a second, then she was waddling back into the room, shaking out the tiny mercury tube away from her. Interesting combination of shapes, like a wombat holding a praying mantis.

"Now put this under your tongue and close your mouth. No talking." No problem, I thought. She turned to me. "And you drink your tea." She poured a cup of rusty brown herbal and left me to occupy myself. The thermometer was held up to the light, with such suspense that even I was leaning in to see what it read. Finally she turned.

"How long have you had this fever?"

"I don't know."

"I think, Hilda, that it just came on during the service."

"Are you sick?"

"I don't think so."

She looked at me. "I wouldn't be too sure about that. Get your hat, Father. This boy has a fever of 110."

✟

He was kept overnight. We left around 11:30. It had been a wearing experience, getting in touch with his parents (well, father, who gave permission for whatever we thought best), filling out forms, and signing things, signing things. I didn't know much about children's illness, but the urgency with which his high temperature was met was impressive. By the time I got to bed, I was more than ready for it.

But once I was there, I found that I couldn't sleep. It was a kind of in-between state, where the voices of dreams are so loud that they snap your eyes open, the immediate reality and the dream reality calamitous. My father's voice was as close as my own breath, and I could see his eyes in my room. *"What do you think you're doing? Break your mother's heart! Twenty-five, I don't care, don't ever step foot in my house again!"* My heart lurched. It was only my bedroom. "St. Augustine had it. Dilation of the blood vessels." Who was that? I fought for wakefulness. I saw the crucifix on the wall beside the bed, silver cast. Expensive, but not extremely well done. I looked closely at the thorns in the crown. No inkling of pain there. One of the thorns looked longer than the rest. Then the next did. They were all elongating, growing, piercing the skin and pushing deep. His eyes opened, and he looked up, his mouth twisting in agony. His head dropped sideways and he stared straight at me, his mouth opening and emitting a long, searing scream.

I was sitting up, wide awake now, and close to hyperventilating. The room was dark, and it took a minute for the shapes to become familiar. The crucifix was there, stable, cast silver, same as always. Good God! I stayed that way until my breath slowed down and became regular again, and my heart quit racing against my chest. The digital clock read 2:17. I brought my feet round to the floor and put on my robe.

By three I had it. In the pages of a cloth-covered hardback. *Incendium amoris:* the mysterious phenomena of the body temperature raising beyond reasonable and rational explanation. St. Philip Neri walked through the winter streets of Rome bare-chested. St. Mary Madgalend Pazzi suffered intolerably from this, tearing her habit and dousing herself with water. It is claimed that in 1923 Foggia, a young Capuchin priest, caused clinical thermometers to break, so high was his temperature. The Dominican nun Maria Villani reportedly emitted a sizzling sound when she drank. This sound could also be heard when water was poured over Venerable Agnes of Jesus*.

I was struck by how close his experience was to that of St. Teresa of Avila. Like her, he was frightened, and at the mercy of these visions, unable to control them. Still, he bore it all out with unwavering tolerance. While the great St. Teresa

---

* *The Eagle and the Dove*, page 5.

had been subjected to like and much worse—for the Devil had once thrown her down a staircase, breaking her arm, to give only one example—the difference was that he never once complained, never thought that perhaps it was too much to bear. She had begged for mercy and release from the distress the overlap of the otherworld caused her. Tommy was meek and submissive about it all, and, in view of his tumultuous inner life, notably good-natured. Although I shouldn't have, I found myself measuring others against him, those whom I knew to be in troubled states, because they had either told me so in confidence, or because they weren't capable of keeping anything in confidence. Indeed, he gave me good example with my minor inconveniences and irritants.

I sighed and closed the book. What was it about him? What was he really? Some freak from the psychotherapy reject pile? An introvert with fervor gone awry? No. I knew, I knew in my heart of hearts, that he was something extraordinary. Greatness graced my confessional chamber, and uttered its secrets to me. He was apart from us. He was so completely advanced in his faith and his heavenly connection that the world would suddenly unfold if it knew what we had here. He was more than human. *He was a saint.* If there was one thing I knew, that I believed in with all my intuition and rationality, if there was anything left that I believed in, this was it.

It was horrible. I knew it had to come sooner or later, but not, please why now? I stared at the letter, not touching it, keeping a space between it and me as if it would separate our worlds.

Dear Father Mulcarthy:
We are pleased to inform you that the Church of Saint Benedict is currently being evaluated for renovation. This will entail upgrading in nearly every facet of the building;

heating and cooling systems, plumbing, ventilation, and facial uplifting. We request that you contact us as soon as possible to arrange an initial consultation with our construction and design heads. We look forward to beginning the creation of the new St. Benedict.

>   Yours in Christ,
>   Raymond Parks and Agatha Beumont;
>   Council of Renovation
>   Vicar General; John Dardioni
>   Diocesan Bishop; Gregory McQueen †

The paper was gleaming white, glaring, in fact. I closed my eyes. We were the last to be hit. By keeping quiet and inconspicuous, I had kept St. Benedict out of the fireraid. Now the ruthless hands of the plows were in the distance, ready to overturn and chew up every bit of the majesty that we still had, the unfathomable beauty of the church. I knew it would hit eventually. I just wasn't prepared. I never would have been. I never would be.

The communion rail… Cream darkly-veined marble, heavy but graceful columns spaced out along its definite straight lines of kneeler and banister… Solid and uninterrupted, joined in the middle by the thick, intricate grillwork of curls and vines. Two angels knelt facing one another in the center of the pattern, knitting the doors shut with their prayers and two golden clasps, fitting perfectly into lock. The sanctuary floor was black and white diamond-slanted checkerboard, flecked and regal with the markings of the marble. IHS laid in a shield in the center, with a long diamond lay of mahogany marble. I loved it all, the Baroque extravagance, the unspeakable beauty, the sheer elegance of the Corinthian pillars as they reached high into the heavens, wrapped by graceful angels swooning in their ascent, the trumpets and harps—yes, harps!—so immediate that the music poured into the dome, swam among the haloed busts of the twelve apostles peering over the gold rim, sailed into the never-ending fresco of our Holy Mother, enraptured in her gaze, reaching a glowing hand of peace through the snow of rosy cherubs bouncing and dipping around her. Red-robed St. Peter struck his muscular arm out into the clouds, piercing and pinning the emerald-green monstrosity below him, a bulbous and strangely handsome snake of thick and strong tail, hissing up at him through cobra-like fans. Peter's wings stretched with the greatest of power, his wild gold hair streaming out like the sun, licking at the milky toes of angels, and tips of their feathery wings, the clouds fading in and out until they gathered in a fantastic wave around the feet, the perfect feet, the feet with the blackened scars. His robe fell like silk, the white pure light of sunrise, disappearing behind the brilliant wash of the rays. The rays came from the heart, the bold and beating heart, entrenched by ebony thorns. Ruby blood poured from it, a cascade too thick and voluminous for one to imagine the source. Blood flowed from the hands, and the crown round the head, flowed into the sky, filling golden chalices studded with diamonds and tanzanite and sapphire, it ran in rivers over bats and vermin, drowning them in its bubbling vat of goodness, conquering all things reptilian and amphibian. The slime underneath dissipated, leaving the shadows of the eternally burning damned waving feebilishly toward heaven to evaporate into nothing, or rather, in some unfathomably intricate design, into Christ's pedestal, over which He smilingly presided. The picture was a riot of color, a symphony of genius, so rich in detail that one could marvel at it for a hundred years and never realize it all.

This dome was the cap to the arcking shrine of the treasure beneath it, the crucifix. Hellenistic, perfect in every detail, the eyes of the suffering Christ closed in such repose that one might consider it sleep, were it not for the brows that were slightly upturned together. The lines of his thin arms cut cleanly the detail the three deltoids, and the biceps, wiry though they were, the scant beard tracing just the right amount of focus up from the precisely-ribbed chest. The loincloth skirted in a graceful diagonal, if not entirely practical, wholly aesthetically pleasing. The legs curved naturally in their demure crossing, leading, with true attention, to the massive, jutting spikes rising from the feet. Three times larger than life at least, it was entirely unique in one thing: the body, Corpus Christi, was carved of marble. The cross itself was pure wood, a dense, heavy fibered wood called iron wood. It remained one of the last true signatures of sheer mastery in art wedded with the Church. It was an icon, it was an era, it was a consummation of all that the faith stood for and rested upon. No amount of labor could reproduce this.

The tabernacle beneath it gleamed in gold, the plates of the doors depicting the five mysteries, each plate set off by ivory Doric columns, the entire piece a kingdom of opulence. Deep purple was the altar cloth before it, laying over the tiny square of marble inlaid into the high altar in which was imbedded a tiny bit of bone from St. Benedict, our resident relic.

The side altars were, though not a drastic break, a definite descent from the pinnacles of these works. The statues of the Holy Mother on the left and St. Benedict on the right were carved with the utmost of craftsmanship, but somewhere along the line, as was often the case, they had been painted, and here was where the flaws lay. The faces lose their dimension when being transferred from sculpture to painting, the eyes lying flat against the remarkably peach skintone, the mouth blatant as a mannequin's. But I was, after all, more skeptical than most about these things, and many an otherwise credible art critic had I heard look upon them with favor, or rather, as was entirely understandable, be so overwhelmed with the magnitude of the entire church and its masterpieces that they overlooked this.

Gone, it would be. This was what had been happening in nearly every church all across the country since Vatican II. The Pope aptly summed up the entire event with the Italian word *Aggiornamento*, meaning updating. As a result of Vatican Council II, the Church was completely restructured, from each document to central Catholic attitudes. Pope John XXIII opened the council in 1962. Between '62 and '65, four sessions were held each autumn, resulting in sixteen documents of reconstruction, covering everything from permission for Catholics to be cremated to the Decree on the Missionary Activity of the Church. The Mass was changed from Latin to the multitudinous vernacular of Christendom. The distinction of ordinal and cardinal sins all fell to the wayside. The study of the Old Testament receded to make way for the New, which became riddled with key signal words like Good News, the new fundamental idea and the vernacular term for the New Testament. Good News, in itself, was the idea that Christ had died and redeemed us, so that we are saved. This in no way precluded the idea of hell and damnation, however, and this dichotomy of emphasis and language is one of the chief sources of misunderstandings I have with people, always, from my boys on up, the same paradoxical problem for both of them, only from different perspectives. The older the person, the closer his upbringing was to the old way, and his puzzlement from the point of damnation out. The boys were raised, so to speak, through the goodness-and-light approach, and are really perplexed by the occasional mention that they could burn in eternal hellfire very easily. Strictions relaxed, and more freedoms were to be found, with the bringing of the Church and Christ home, into the hearts and the homes. Converts liked the idea of everyone for one and one for one, namely Christ, but this new Christ, the one who could be shaped according to their desires. He applied to the individual. Sin disappeared and with it went the sense of moral duty, of fiber, of the possibility of doing wrong, the danger of injuring another, and of the responsibility for transgression, because everyone is right about religion as long as the religion they choose is Catholicism, for starters, and as long as it includes ten percent of the earnings falling weekly into the collection basket. The new carnival atmosphere looked more attractive to those with time on their hands and baking ability, hence was born the new stereotype: the churchlady. Volunteers flourish, virtually, as everyone likes a nice plate of cake or a youth group ordering pizza, and no one has to worry about making an act of contrition. It is not necessary, really, to learn this or any other prayers, anymore, because whatever you say will be fine, if it is from your heart. Gone are tradition and mysticism out the window with clowns for Christ. Don't laugh; I've seen them, and the dignity that the Church once knew became poisoned with felt cut-out banners of suns and rainbows. All the image of a God who was apart from man, not only in proximity, but in character, was swept away to make room for the man of Jesus, who only lost his temper once in a den of thieves. "I AM A VENGEFUL GOD" was a forgotten line, although it was said just as long ago and even longer than the other archaisms that became the few flashcard catechism rites to being a Catholic. Come unto me, Hear the Good News, Welcome the Kingdom of God. Wasn't it good, you ask, that more people were brought to the Church? No! Whatever makes you think that everyone is cut out to be a Catholic? It is a privilege and an honor. It is said that non-Catholics lack the "gift of faith." Not everyone is cut out for eternal life. The Blessed are the few, the chosen. These new Catholics are not offered the Holy Church, as it has been known and acknowledged for centuries; they are offered something completely different, something quick and obligation-free, which requires no serious thought or study. Something vital was gone, something that had called attention of grown men and embittered women, something had that caused families over the world to kneel down in their homes and venerate a crucifix. Gone was something that lawyers of the country could call upon the basest criminal in court to realize that he had done wrong, and should be afraid, something that gave the Church power. There was something that was cast in tradition, something that endured and was known across the spans of time and culture and language and land, something that all people need to know in their hearts and their souls if they are to live their lives as decent human beings, nevermind the divine: are they aware that they themselves are not the center of the universe, that they are connected with something bigger than themselves, and that everything they do and say and think is of consequence and has effect, namely in the consequence of eternal damnation or deliverance? Do they realize that they themselves are nothing in the grand scheme of things, nothing in the sense of their mortality? They will die, and this will go on, this all will go on, whatever this happens to be, and nothing they do can ever change that.

This seems an irony, but in fact, it is not. It is a perfect balance of principles. Everything you do effects something in the chain. But in viewing the entire chain, nothing you do is of any significance. Your actions matter in your own destiny, but not the world's. While you are here, you must be responsible. Your own glories and tribulations will not endure here. Something larger will.

✝

His fever had completely disappeared at midnight, they said. He was released without any conclusive explanation of the mysterious overheating. As they hadn't really done anything for him, I couldn't see the use of taking him back when it recurred, as it did—every Friday without fail, from evening until midnight, the precise starting time eventually settling into 6:00pm. I only hoped that Mother Superior wouldn't take notice, and, as Tom was invariably in the church during these fevers, she had no occasion to take notice. I certainly didn't bring it to her or Hilda's or anyone else's attention after that first instance. Tom knew what was causing the spells, and so did I.

They wasted no time. When I met with the committee to renovate St. Benedict's, there was no request for any input from me whatsoever. The plans had been drawn out, and exacted, with a complete budget that very carefully extracted just the amount from us that we could let go without a strain, the personnel lined up and the schedules figured up. My weekend schedule would be altered, the one that had remained untouched for 42 years: Saturday evening liturgies would move from 5:00 to 7:00, to allow for a full day of construction; and Sunday morning lost a Mass altogether, unless I wanted to hold it outside, weather-permitting. The 8:00 a.m. Mass would move back to 7:00 a.m., the 10:00 to 9:30, and noon was discontinued. This was not to be thought of as any way permanent; I was free to change it back or to whatever I liked once the remodeling was finished. How many people I would lose with the new schedule, I could only imagine. Who has the gall to change a noon Mass of twenty years' duration? Nevermind that Sunday is the Lord's Day and a day of rest. I didn't even bother to bring it up. It was an obvious point, and it was obviously being overlooked. Construction would be ongoing and daily, beginning in two weeks. So much for the peace and the serenity of the open church for the person with an hour in an odd time of day to spend alone in contemplation. Such moments would be under siege from denim-covered workmen whirring drills, passing over one another with two-by-fours, and filling the air with plaster dust. A refuge, our sanctuary would not be. The daily Mass would be moved from 8:00 a.m. to 7:30. While 7:00 would be considered most convenient, they didn't want to overload me with a new early-morning rising schedule. As for the little extra things we did, such as confessions, holy hour, veneration of the Holy Host in the Monstrance, vespers, etc., they were left to my discretion.

The church itself… A new backbone, that's what it needed. It was, let's face it, forgotten in the march of technological progress and could shine in the light of modern advancements.

New plumbing (no more thumps and banging), new heating (good-bye hissing radiators), insulation, and a more efficient window system were among the improvements. These changes would be accomplished by a whole new inner structure, if you will, of the church body itself. New, fortified inner walls would allow for the insulation. The old windows, which, though a fine example of Byzantine icons, are, in fact, completely impractical for heating purposes, and do not meet all the fire codes, with their simple and meager iron framework. The most advanced system incorporated the windows into the walls themselves, so as not to detract the aesthetic line. They could be slender, and sleek, now, in keeping with the new design, with less graphic depictions than St. Job flocked by dogs licking his wounds, and Christ in despair over the rock at Gethsemene. In fact, the entire idea would be something more representational of sentiment, as could be achieved only by the fine art of the abstract. This gave far more freedom for uniformity in design, concepts and expressions by way of color, and shape, which, after all, are more likely to evoke feelings from the onlooker. One artist's harsh realism is only appealing to a select audience, while evocative suggestions can be interpreted any number of ways and means, according to the individual. The message should be able to fit whatever their needs happen to be at the time. So, slender and subtle, the windows would be thoroughly sealed and airtight with a wide runner of a new black plastic-like material, each with a small square at the bottom which swivels out for ventilation, if desired, but, as you will see, in the face of the new ventilation system including gas cooling and ceiling fans, such reliance on the unpredictable outside elements is really minimal, if anything. Beyond that, the windows are a permanent fixture, a streak of decor in the wall, designed not to overpower, but to subtly complement, and need no more notice than the occasional typical cleaning. Walls will be between a creme and a light beige stucco. Simple miniature gas sconces will add a sparse decorative touch.

Carpet. As the new color motif is natural browns, the carpet will be a thin, tightly woven pile of almond. This will cover everything, from the vestibule to the altar. It is the utmost in stain-resistance and low-maintenance, absorbs sound, and, again, is less distracting, drawing more attention to the people on it than the floor itself. The sanctuary floor will be lowered when the marble is removed, so the entire church floor will be level. This breaks down that level between the priest and the congregation, and makes them feel more a part of the liturgy. It also makes the priest seem more like one of them. For that matter, the communion rail will be taken out.

New pews will allow for greater comfort. More like theatre seats, the frames will be of durable steel, and the covering a tight synthetic tan wool. This is easily advantageous over the present oak, which bows and otherwise suffers with age, with some, though grant it, not many, splits, and of course the defacing that wood is subjected to. The backs are hinged with a plastic sleeve for hymnals and the like. No kneelers will be installed. In the new Mass, kneeling is not really necessary, and for many, physically not practical, and those should not feel limited in God's house from paying proper homage. The new design will be further practical, in that every pew will now be handicapped accessible, with the added legroom that the kneelers denied.

The side altars are not a current practice in Holy Mother Church. But Bernie's has such beautiful statues in its, that after careful consideration, it was decided that the structures of the sides can remain. On left altar, where the statue of Mary is now, will stand both the statues of Mary and Benedict, with a new gift of a brass lamb to sit at their feet. It compliments the gold in the paint and had been donated by a very prestigious patron on the east coast. These figures will all be moveable so that their display can be rotated with, for example, a manger scene at Christmastime. The votive candles naturally must go.

From the right altar, where Bernie was, the tabernacle will

go. Actually, it is not the present tabernacle, as it is a bit rich for the motif, but a modern cherrywood cylinder with minimal line carvings on the sides. It may have one thin white candle, although this should only be used for actual services. The traditional sanctuary candle will be replaced by an ingenious new electric device which can double as a candleholder, and which follows fire code and flickers in imitation of a real candle flame.

The crucifix, rather a morbid centerpiece to focus on, will be replaced by the figure of the risen Christ, carved from wood in simple and bold design by Agatha Beumont. Her work is extraordinary, as all must agree, and the statements she makes with absolute minimalism are both striking and memorable. The dome will have to go. The new inner structure includes a new lowered ceiling in connection with the new walls, the result being a drawing together of the congregation in a closer space, far more efficient and continuous, with the unbroken wash of cream stucco.

That's it, the entire design, innovative and inspiring as it is. The committee has worked hard to put together the most energy-efficient and uplifting design that is practical for all of St. Benedict's special needs, finishing outside with ramps and expanded driveway through the wild space beyond the present parking lot. And Agatha has agreed to incorporate the wood from those very trees into as many of the designs as possible. Right now, she has some exciting ideas for holy water fonts from that wood. All in all, everyone must agree, that exactly one year from now, the area will be amazed with the illustrious new Church of St. Benedict, the utmost in high-impact simplicity.

☩

What I needed was a Scotch. I could see the glass before me plain as the inside of my eyelids, the pale caramel color interrupted only by the fewest lumps of ice. Yet here I was, in the dark confessional, waiting out a quiet night of the excusable and mundane. I wouldn't have even minded just talking to people. In fact, I wished I were in a position to do so. Listening, this was what was required of me now, and it would be over soon enough. Then Hilda could fix me that Scotch and I would go to bed. I had an accomplice to a real embezzler, that night, as I remember. It is strange how we always get the accomplices, but not the serious offenders. There were droughts between the repentant and the perplexed, and finally I was comforted to hear the soft steps of my boy, the same cadence and gentility he had entered with two years ago. About halfway into the confession, his voice started to grow heavy, rounder.

"The parting of the sky, dripping red and pink, washes away the cold whiteness of the day. Leave me to it, Lord, Take me in it, Lord. Your Will be done."

Was it me and my present state, or was he being ominous? It all seemed out of focus, tonight; I had only arrived back from the bomb-drop meeting an hour ago. I knew I could be of no help to him now, if indeed I ever had been. A saint in the midst of the holocaust. Imagine.

He was drifting. I put my hand on the grate, palm toward him, imagining I could feel his heat beginning with the twilight of Friday evening. His eyes would be closed. I closed mine. His mystery began, and we were together.

·✝·

Two weeks, and the plowing had begun. The new Mass schedule was chaos in the air, palpable as any thunderstorm over an unsuspecting picnic. Attendance was scatty and transient, and Hilda made sure that she was in sight of the Church at noon, to redirect those who hadn't yet heard, or had simply forgotten. They came with huge trucks and drastic tools which I tried to ignore, like jackhammers and crowbars. A small committee had formed and recorded St. Benedict's before the renovation began, on video and hundreds of photographs, including all the vessels and vestments.

Tarpaulins and scaffolding became fixtures as resigned to infinite existence as the statues had been. Why it all moved so slowly, who could say? Why did any construction seem to take the eternity of God's own funeral dirge, dragging on and on and on? Easter had just ended a week ago, and there had been a mad scramble to remove all the lilies, palms, and endless candles that had filled the Church and restore it to the orderly cleanliness of ordinary time. The linens and altar cloths again were white, the handsomeness of the bare marble showing through where brimming baskets of flowers and silks had been. No one was pleased, of course. There were outcries in all forms and levels, from the inconvenience to the immorality of it all. I shouldn't say that none were pleased. That isn't true. New groups were beginning to form, to be sure their names were connected with the historical transition, no doubt, and especially new parishioners were genuinely excited. But I wasn't exposed to these as often, and certainly didn't pay them as much mind, as those who were raising cock-ups. There was no concept that I was powerless here, as I had been on the committee of renovation. (This fact was included in the announcement in the bulletin from the bishop.) I was pastor, after all. On the contrary, I was all but held responsible. It was a constant barrage of outcry, confusion, question, and most intolerably, opinion, opinion, opinion, opinion. You know, even if it happened to coincide with my own, I didn't want to hear it. And yet all I could do was utter one perpetual line of consolation and assurance that this what was the Church wanted, this was the will of the Holy Father, and the Church must grow in keeping with the times. There are those who know more than we.

Appointments were scheduled increasingly, interviews with area newspaper reporters, and the television news station, individual freelance writers looking for an exclusive for this and that and the other. Suddenly the mailbox was flooded with query letters and portfolios from artists wanting to work on the project, and laborers, long-time out of work, searching for a job. The trustees, although we shouldn't call them by that name, our supporters, were an insatiable void needing answers and discussions and figures, if not together, then separately, in lunches, dinners, and long car rides in the country. Only three didn't require such treatment, out of seventy-five major contributors. That I was exhausted goes without saying. For that matter, so was Hilda, who suddenly found herself chief hostess and receptionist for the parade. I felt sorry for her. Rough as she sometimes was, she was a good person who worked very earnestly and with honest intentions for me. She had never been in the heat of such excitement, and I thought she was handling it like a champ. I had a few lunches catered, just to take the pressure off, and tried to redirect as much of my work and errands as possible, through the secretaries and everyone else on staff. Things had gone on so long unchanged that this came as a complete shock to everyone's systems, and it didn't help matters that the week of Palm Sunday, the hard drive crashed in the central computer system. What had once been so stable was now Pandemonium.

I turned out the light and stared at the square neon green numbers glowing on the alarm clock. Only hours until the world would start up again.

✠

He walked into the darkened church. Only the flicker of the sanctuary candle and the faintest hints of moonlight remained to guide him. The new framework erected inside the walls was slowly overtaking the side aisles, as they now stood, and he walked in the main aisle. No one was inside. He knelt at the rail, the silence a strange intermission in a place so bombarded with sound. He stared at the crucifix, the skeleton beneath the marble skin as evident as his own. It was the second Friday of Lent, and the evening stations had been cancelled, the sculptured tableaus of the stations of the cross all but invisible behind the new wood. He fell into the heaviest stillness, limbs frozen and unflinching, the chest unmoving under his t-shirt. The time went by, slowly, the candle growing higher and higher in the night, the wax streaming its almost imperceptible air of beeswax and sulphur. A shadow passed through the vestibule and paused.

✠

There was a knock at the door. An unkempt man in thin overalls smoothed his hair back and was let in to wait in the outer office. After a time, the door opened.

"Hello, I am the Mother Superior."

He looked unsteadily at her until she heralded him toward a seat across from her desk. She waited.

"Hi. I'm, my name is Louis Macintyre, I'm on the crew next door, and I used to be Catholic." He fidgeted.

"Yes?"

"Well, I thought I should tell you, last night I was in the church later than the guys, I was in late, and . . . well, I saw something strange, and I want to tell somebody. So I thought, hey, the nuns were in charge when I was in church, so maybe they still are now, and-"

"What is it that you saw, Mr. Macintyre?"

"Well, you, you'll think I'm kinda out there when I tell you this, I mean, I know what's what and when a guy sounds nuts."

"What did you see, Mr. Macintyre?"

"There wasn't nobody there, see, when the guys went, so I come walking upstairs from the kitchen, and, there was this kid up front at the railing, kneeling down."

"Yes?"

"Well, he seemed to be praying pretty hard, so I didn't want to disturb him, you know. So I walk away, and when I come back up, sure he's gonna be gone, he's still there, and he's kneeling, but one thing, see—he's floating up in the air."

"I beg your pardon?"

"Yea, see, I knew it would sound crazy, but there he was, swear to Christ—oh, excuse me—and he was about a foot off the ground. I went down to take a piss, and when i came back, he was gone."

"I see."

"Yea. Look, I know you don't want to believe me, but there he was, honest to God, in the air, I ain't kidding you. I do take this stuff seriously sometimes still, you know."

"And what did this kid look like?"

"A kid. Maybe fifteen, maybe twenty, I don't know. T-shirt and jeans."

"What color was his hair?"

"Hair? Oh, well, about blonde, I guess. And oh yea, he had one of them pieces that stick up right in front, like this." He pulled a lock of his own hair up in front of his forehead, straight into the air.

"Is that it?"

"It? Yea, that's all. He was gone after that."

She grunted. "Well, thank you, Mr. Macintyre. I appreciate your concern. I'll take care of it from here."

She stood, and so did he. "What are you gonna do? You know who it is?"

"I'll take care of it. Good day, now."

"Yea, o.k., good day. Hey, nice talking to you. Swell office you got here."

She closed the door behind him, and went to the phone.

"Hello, Hilda. Is Father there? Mmm. Have him call me the minute he gets in."

✟

"It's not a good idea to have shenanigans going on around here with all the attention we already have from the press. Whatever he's up to, you have to put a stop to it."

"What do you propose that I do?" This was all I needed.

"I don't know what he's up to, and i don't know what you're up to. But you're the only one who seems to be able to talk to him, and that makes it your place to take the reigns. He has been nothing but trouble for me since day one."

"Mother, we have been through this and through this until we've talked ourselves blue. He hasn't been a single bit of trouble for you, and you know it. He sets the standard for the other boys. Anyway, I don't see what your fretting about, and I don't see what you want me to do."

"No one is going to listen to a fourth-grade education carpenter ape, so there's nothing to be done that way just now. But I've had it with all the attention our quiet church and school has had from all this renovation business anyway, and if this is some kind of publicity stunt -"

At that moment, something in me snapped. "Is that what you're driving at? You may be the head nun here. You may be the pope, for all I care, but I am telling you now, that I have had it with your insubordination, and your accusations, and your condemnation of my judgment and character, and far moreover, that boy's. If a quieter atmosphere is what you want, a quieter atmosphere is what you've got!"

I rose out of my own office and left her, gaping and spellbound, in the echo of my last words. I got into my car and drove as quickly as I legally could through the city and out of it, passing into the sparser slums of the city's outskirts, staring past the falling porches and the indoor furniture become lawn furniture with the afternoon's collection of skinny neighborhood dogs. I saw the peeling paint, I smelled the illegal fires in backyards, keeping my window rolled up, because hearing the vagrant clusters of out of school children making their din across the grey sky was one thing I did not want to do, but the rest was fine. Broken fences, crumbling buildings, gone from coffee houses and department stores to housing projects and empty shells. Funny, no graveyards, but trashcans sometimes tumbled into the street, in pursuit of the spill of papers and beer cans run once again amuck, stopped cars that had remained unmoved for the life of fads, and novelties, for the life of the young man who had been shot in that corner bar, it was all here, the debauched and inescapable nuclei, who never left and never would, the stability of the curiously indifferent and embittered, forever encased behind these grafittied brick walls.

I kept driving, feeling the lull of the engine as it changed gears, unconsciously shifting my gaze from the road to the green glow of the digital time. When I caught myself doing it, I shut it off immediately. The lots grew wider, the forgotten half-gravel being swallowed into the mouth of the wild grasses, the muted browns and straws becoming fuller as I drove further on, trees coming into view, trees that had grown of their own accord, unlike those of the city. The sky was beginning the faintest paling through the thin covering of stratus clouds drawing out the light behind them, a slow leak onto a dirty grey tablecloth. I had absolutely no sense of destination and felt the crunch of dirt road under the tires. I eased up on the accelerator and coasted for a while, letting the odd angles of headstones fill my vision. White, off-white, ash, dark grey, occasional rose they called rose which wasn't rose at all. The shine dulled away as I entered the older section, with its slender slabs of weathering, careful lettering, the grass beginning to tell who was visited and who was not. I stopped the car and got out, my legs appreciative of the stretch. A long way we had come. The air was crisp.

It's a good feeling, to walk in a cemetery. No sense of rush, no hint of it at all, a retreat oft overlooked and forgotten. They were secure and solitary, inviting private musings with promises of their confidence. Stone after stone told another name gone, another date to be put in the past. A chipmunk looked at me as if I was a foreigner, and was gone. Well, I guess I am. Infants, 'Our Thomas,' 'Little Alah' . . . there were so many in the older times. I used to walk through as a boy, and try to guess all the nationalities, which were immigrants and which were natives; figure how long one spouse had outlasted another. Mostly it was the women who did. I would be easily snobbish to those with extravagant memorials. I stopped at a rectangular grave, sunk into the ground, grass growing untended round the edges. Stephan Mulcarthy. Well, Dad, how are you? Here's your lost son, come round now that you're safe under. I looked up at the mulberry bush a little beyond, and the scant impatience someone had pressed into the ground. They never seemed to look natural, these flowers, no matter where they were. Generic. So, is this what you were trying to warn me about? Too bad you missed it. You really would have gotten a rise out of it, all of this. *Throwing your life away,* you said. *Worthless sack, that's what'll become of you, you do it. Bunch of money-hungry liars.* Funny how the worst of words have the most indelible mark on the memory. And now here I am, a good serviceman, as far as my duties go, a man of the cloth who can't remember where he put God. He used to be there, whenever this young self-pitying man was wallowing about his deplorable homelife, too cowardly to straighten his backbone and begin something. He was there, in the quiet of the church way far on the other side of town, away from his troubles and sleepless nights. He was there, when the young man asked Him if he was worthy to answer His call. The vibrant young deacon who knew theology better than he had any girl's body, who walked in without a backward glance and cried for joy at the feeling that what he was doing was finally *right. I*t was *right;*, it was exactly and completely the thing to do. He swore his life over to Christ and was home, in the guts and the bottom of his soul and belief. I haven't kept the photographs; Mother got them and framed or matted every one in a $45.00 leather-bound album. Where they went when she died, I lost track. It wasn't important to me. What was important was that one Christmas she showed them to me, over some monstrous plate of cinnamon rolls I had loved as a boy, but which were sickeningly sweet now, and I was struck by how happy I looked. My eyes had a light, a light from deep within, my face was relaxed and handsome, and young, young for the first time; I didn't recognize myself.

Maybe where the young man is, God is there too, wondering when I'm going to drop in. The thing is, that I didn't know exactly when they left; I never had. One would expect a cataclysm, material for some big dramatic soliloquy, about the very moment when I realized it was all leaving. A sign, a billboard, a memento, something. The truth was that it was such a gradual departure that it was entirely natural, nothing notable at all. Here I was and of course where else would I be? Yes, what a snide laugh you'd get out of all of this, Dad, your son the failed priest. Should have stuck around; they say the evil never die.

I breathed hard and felt my shoulders catch something in my back, some muscle. The air was beginning to feel brisk now, and night would be here in a little while. I looked up into the branches of an oak and walked over to it, sitting down. I drew my knees in and laid down, the roots just framing my curled form.

✠

His Fast of forty days
makes this a holy season of self-denial.
By rejecting the devil's temptations
He has taught us
to rid ourselves of the hidden corruption of evil,
and so to share his paschal meal in purity of heart,
until we come to its fulfillment
*in the promised land of heaven.**

---

* *New Latin-English Sunday Missal,* 1983, page 107.

I can't take all the credit for it. She had been in blatant opposition to the renovation and, moreover, the upgrades in the Mass and the relaxing of the stricter teachings. Nevertheless, in two months, she was gone. The quieter reaches of small-town Idaho had a sudden need for an assistant to the Mother Superior to chaperone the all-girl catholic high school, consisting of seventy-five students total, and she was called upon to fill the void. I considered her final Lent with us my penance.

She reminded me of the old nuns, the ones who slapped hands with paddles for holding pens incorrectly and forced students to kneel in front of the radiator and say the rosary for being late to school on a winter's day. I did know that at interschool dances, she still tried to make the students kneel on the gym floor and recite a Hail Mary if they had an impure thought. This didn't work out well, for obvious reasons, so instead of waiting for the kids to figure out whether they were having impure thought, she would decide it for them and stand over them while the prayer was said under the party lights. Well, she was older, and came from a time when this was the way things were done, and I couldn't really fault her for it. In fact, I never had occasion to; a month before I signed on at St. Benedict's, the general vicar (at the time) himself had been witness to this practice during a visit to the school that was being recorded by all the area religious media, and it had come to an abrupt—and silent—halt. No one really would have cared otherwise, and no one raised a whimper about her gestapo tactics at the school other than the students. Sometimes they raised an out and out wail, but they really didn't have much of an audience. Most immediately, there's me, and I encourage forbearance. Discipline is an important part of the faith. Being raised in it, the impact is all the more certain to be made and if it gets carried a bit too far.

Anyway, this was something I really don't feel I have a claim to. One missing part of my Catholicism that is very real to me is not being raised Catholic. I have a theory on converts of any kind: on one hand, they have in their favor that their involvement is by choice, and generally, they will know more about their religion than the Cradle Catholics themselves, out of both actual requirement to know in initiation, and out of zeal and hunger for the knowledge. Their sentiment is powerful and devotion strong. On the other hand, there is something they can never have, and that is the experience of being raised in this (new) religion, the ingrained, basic programming and training that one who has it takes for granted. That is so much a part of him that it cannot be divorced from his early experience, nor can he probably ever fully realize the extent of its influence on his thinking patterns, decisions, reactions, metaphors, words, disposition, organization of perception, etc., etc., etc. This interwoven fiber can never be possessed by one past his early years. The same things can be learned and processed, but the experience can never be had. Furthermore, the pratfall of a convert is that he has the tendency to become overzealous about his new religion, and quite frankly, a bore about the subject.

Catholic converts have a particular loophole: ongoing radical changes in teaching and attitudes. There is no peg-holing their conversion experience; there's no telling what they're learning. Before Vatican II, when I made my conversion, the program was extensive. Besides weighty and rigorous study, we converts were denied certain privileges in the church; for example, an announcement was made by the priest at the point of the beginning of the transubstantiation, when the bread and the wine would be changed into the body and the blood of Christ, that all candidates for conversion must now leave the church. It was quite some time before we were permitted to actually witness this miracle. Consequently, many new converts could be seen riveted to the process once they were allowed in, while the seasoned veterans ranged from, granted, devout attention, to, more to the point, being nudged awake.

So, you see, this whole era and upbringing of the infamous extreme measures of nuns in the education system was something outside of my experience. Catholics had known and endured it for centuries. Who was I to question? She wasn't as radical as many legends I heard tell of about other nuns; she hadn't broken any bones or made anyone bleed. No, I take that back; Jacob Stansky had been caught eating a hamburger on Good Friday once perhaps twelve years ago, and she had whipped his stomach with his own regulation leather belt until, well, I'm sure, if he's married, he had some explaining to do to his wife. And he apparently had only sinned out of forgetfulness.

The whole of Lent passed with a trying air. Parishioners grew a little more settled in the idea of transition, although divisions seemed to be being drawn between those who supported the changes and those who opposed them, with subdivisions according to their reasons. I should add that the main changes lay only in the renovation project; this wasn't, after all, the tide of Vatican II. We weren't just changing from Latin to English or the priest to a position facing the faithful. The minor revisions I resisted were the optional ones. I still genuflected before the Host after the miracle, and indeed, genuflected when passing the tabernacle at any time; I favored receiving Communion on the tongue rather than in the hand, to avoid the irreverent and unclean touch; I kept the grate in the confessional instead of holding face-to-face. Still, core old way feelings were tied to the crucifix, the communion rail, the presence of the inactive high altar, and the overall tragic grandeur. This is precisely the reason they had to go. And this was the nerve that was being hit with the stripping of all this. For some, it was like watching their very religion being erased. We couldn't have statues anymore, because they were too often treated like idols, or so the reasoning was. We were lucky to be keeping the two that we had, though they weren't being bolted down. Oh, I was growing so tired.

And then there was Tommy. In the midst of all this, he was a constant, a shadow in the corner of a lightning storm, and I felt bad that I hadn't been able to give him the time that he deserved. He remained indifferent to all of this; I wasn't sure how much of what was happening he understood, or should I say, was aware of. He was so far into his inner secret life of raptures and terrors, visions and voices, that he really seemed to have room for little else. I sighed, realizing that the new Mother Superior would have to be primed for him, the "nightmares," as everyone regarded them, the absent-mindedness, the frequent sickness. Yes, this was something that had steepened, his frequent viruses and unnamable illnesses; Tom spent as much time in bed as out. He was what the Victorians would have called "pale in constitution," and everyone was well accustomed to it. Least of all, it seemed not to attract the concern of Tom; he was never heard to make a complaint and often had to be completely overtaken by an illness before anyone could realize that he was suffering. It happened, though, that the notice of malnutrition attracted more than the suspicious glance from the area hospital, until Mother Superior had gone into the main office herself and made a lengthy and memorable notification that this was not due to the treatment of the students by the staff of St. Benedict's. Well, now. There was something to her credit. I like to think of the public getting their fair dose of the Mother.

Holy Week found Tom down with a tremendous case of bronchitis. Though the boys were naturally out of school for the solemnity, he had stayed on, as he really did belong here rather than Minnesota, and was too ill to be crossing the country. The first chance I got, I stopped in to see him. It was on Tuesday morning. He was gaunt, and sallow in complexion, with shadows of exhaustion and sickness under his eyes. The cowlick was stuck together, as one messy clump, instead of a charming curl. He was asleep. I waited until he woke, the better part of an hour. He looked disorientated at first, as if he couldn't quite pull out of a deep thought, then he saw me. His stare continued, perplexed, for a moment, and then his face relaxed and fell to a vague smile.

"Hello, Tom. How do you feel?"

He nodded, made a sound, cleared his throat, and tried again. "Fine, thanks."

His voice was faint and scratchy. I realized suddenly that there was no excuse for not coming sooner, renovation or not, and sat up straight.

"The work is still going on in the church; they've finished surveying and have the scaffolding up in the rear, inside and out."

"I can see the tarpaulins." I followed his eyes out the window. The tarps hung like mysterious curtains over the outside of the back windows, veils beginning a magic disappearing act.

"I hear you've been around the church at night." He nodded. I wanted to ask him about the levitation but couldn't find a subtle and casual way to do so. I suppose such a subject doesn't often just creep into conversations. "What do you think of the work that's going on, Tom?" It was both a conversational question and an earnest query; I really wanted to know his feelings on it, albeit I could hardly bear to hear any others' anymore.

His eyes closed languidly for a moment. "Doesn't matter." He said.

I was thunderstruck. "Doesn't matter? What do you mean?" I backed up in my thoughts. "Do you know what the result will look like?"

"Yes, the rendering is posted in the vestibule and downstairs in the trophy hall." A sentence of this length was obviously a strain on him. He was trying to catch his breath.

"How can it not matter?" He looked kind. His expression changed to definite focus on a thought.

"Father, do you know that the Lord didn't walk down Calvary at all? It was impossible. They put the beam on his shoulders several times, but it was too heavy. He was weak. So they pushed him with it and kept trying to put it back on. But every time, He fell. He kept falling. He was dying."

I heard the words. They suddenly called me back into the Lenten season. Stations tonight. No, they were cancelled. Well, we still could have held a Holy Hour; why hadn't I thought of that? There was so much to think about.

"This week He remembers, and it is too much to remember; so He gives His memories to others. This is the one He gave to me. I remember. And, Father, the cross is so heavy."

His eyes fluttered. He was tiring. "I love to carry His cross. I love the feel of it on my shoulders and the weight that pushes all the way to my very feet. Sometimes it comes down sharply, and I cannot breathe. That is when He shows me his beautiful face, and the light washes all over me. I forget myself then. I can carry more."

His breath was light and his eyes appeared to have no connection with what his mind was seeing, erratically moving, closing, shifting, dilating and contracting. I could see that he had a fever. "Yes, Lord" he whispered, and I watched with amazement his body bowing, and growing rigid, his shoulders caving in, his neck long and bent. On impulse I pulled the sleeve of his gown, revealing young, bony shoulders, blue and green bruises rising on the skin. His head dropped, devoid of tension, and then went stiff with the rest. I held a body unmalleable as stone, frozen into this distorted arc. I felt for his pulse. Nothing. I panicked and moved my fingers again. Nothing. I grabbed the other wrist and practically jammed my fingers into the spot of the vein, my own heart beating so palpably I feared it would override detection of his. I couldn't find it and put my hand under his gown onto his chest. It was nowhere near as warm as my hand. "Tommy?" I called. "Tommy?" My voice flew away from me, growing louder.

Suddenly my hands were on his shoulders, shaking him, moving the whole frame that would not give, and then his hands shot out in front of him, hands grasping the empty air.

"Oh, my Savior," he whispered. "You have chosen me to help bear the weight of Your sacred cross. I will not fall again." Then he made a huge gasp for air and fell into my arms, limp and without will. He was not conscious. I lowered him back onto the bed but could not let go. My heart would not slow down, and his voice still rang in my ears. I sank onto the side of the bed and grasped him tighter, his shoulders too thin to hide my hot face. My throat caught and my breath jerked. The tears grew strange and full in my shut eyes, pushing their way out, my throat choking out painfully weak sounds that I hadn't heard in years. They came and came, tears that wetted my cheek and my chin, running sloppily over my lips and me pressing them to Tom's neck. I grasped him closer, his short unwashed hair flattened next to mine, my chest pulling inward with each yank of a sob. *Thank You, God; there's no one here,* I thought.

Then his eyes opened. They were so full of love that my tears seemed to come faster, amazed and ashamed in the face of such greatness. His eyes said everything for him and about him. They reached into me, they told me to *be calm. All is well. You are in my arms and all that is good is here, so wide and so big that you can never grasp it. There is such goodness that I cannot begin to glimpse it all, even looking into the Lord's Eyes.* My pain and my upsurge all seemed to be placed on hold for a moment, as those eyes looked on me, a sensation of being uprooted from the place of blackness to sudden light, and all I could do was stare at it, dumbly, wonderingly, like a child. His gaze was steady and unbroken. He didn't blink. Then his eyelids closed halfway, the focus remaining constant, words unspoken. Finally they closed completely. He was plainly asleep. I held him for a moment, looking on at the closed eyes, looking without a single thought, and then backed up, standing, kissing first his right hand and then the other, moving to the foot of the bed and kissing both of his feet. I looked at his crucifix, hung over a tiny hair crack of plaster, like a fly on the wall watching the whole while. I hung my head and tried to look at it but could not hold the gaze. I picked up my coat and left.

✠

The new Mother Superior was due in at 9:00 for breakfast in the rectory. I finished Mass and was on my second cup of coffee, reading over the early Wednesday paper before she arrived. The doorbell rang. I looked at the clock: 8:50. Hilda appeared in a moment. I could hear her voice, very cheerful, through the hall.

"You just come through the back door. It's always open. No need to knock."

I rose. A slim woman, almost as tall as I, with a delicate hand shook mine. "Hello. I am Father Mulcarthy. Have a seat."

"Pleased to meet you. I am Christina Rhodes." There was something different about her, not just that she departed from the regular habit of the nuns here, wearing a tailored navy blue skirt and blouse, but something that roused me out of the complacent mood with which I had prepared myself for this meeting.

"Lovely rectory you have here. This kitchen is so full of light, with the bay window. It's a marvelous spot to breakfast."

"Yes, well, thank you. That's Hilda. This is all her kitchen." Hilda was still standing in the doorway beaming at her. "You've met Hilda? She pretty much runs things around here, really. Anything you need to know about, she's the one to ask. She's indispensable."

"Oh, that's good to know. I had thought as much when we spoke over the phone. I am pleased to meet you."

"Oh, sure. Anything you need, you just call me. I'm always here."

"Thank you."

"Thank you," I said, pausing until Hilda looked at me, realizing that her hostessing was finished.

"Well, I'll let you two eat your breakfast. I'll be in the basement."

We both thanked her, and she was gone.

"Well, Hilda's laid out breakfast for a king here. What can I get you? Coffee?"

"Oh, yes, please, that would be splendid. Cream, no sugar."

I poured her some and refilled my own. Number three, why not.

"So, how've you settled in? Found everything all right?"

She took the coffee with both hands in toward her lap.

"Oh yes, thank you. The wing is very comfortable in the school. I can't wait to meet the boys."

"Oh, well, you may wish that hadn't come so soon." She laughed.

"I understand you have a doctorate."

"Yes, in Philosophy. I attended Vassar. I have been working toward another degree in communications."

"Indeed?"

"Yes. The emphasis is on refining of the English language."

"And what will you do with that?"

She wiped her mouth lightly on the corner of her napkin. "Pretty much all that I've been doing, really, in Our Lady of Divinity. I am on the modern language committee in the heart of the diocese, you see."

"Yes, I remember seeing something like that in your paperwork. You edit things?"

She nodded and continued to flash me her brilliant and strong smile. "We're doing wonderful things downtown." This meant the diocese central. "I teach a seminar for educators and authorities alike in redefining the language. It's most stimulating. Do you enjoy language work?"

I suddenly realized that she was indeed the principal,

and somehow that belated impact and her focused tone made me feel as if I were some dumb kid back in a classroom again, trying to bring himself up from a 'C' in English. "It's interesting. I don't do much about it on my own." I paused. "More coffee?"

"Yes, please. I hope to strengthen St. Benedict's English department, both in composition and literature. Do you realize that the curriculum has remained the same for nearly thirty years?"

So has the old Mother, I thought. "That must be due for a change."

"It's ripe."

I drew on my coffee, realizing that I probably had very little to do with this turnover in the school's staff after all. In fact, it was probably just uncannily convenient that I had made my complaint when I did. She had been sent from upstairs as just another extension of the "upgrading" of St. Benedict's. She was prime cut: modern, strong, progressive, charming, and evidently good. Besides her extensive education, which included study in Rome and an internship in New York editing a feminist rag, which I had been waiting for her to mention, she was right this moment pleasantly and skillfully laying the ground for her real plans. All I had to do was sit and wait and say Mass on my own side of the allotment. I smiled at her.

"So what plans do you have for the school?" I took the bull by the horns, or something by the horns.

"Well," she swallowed and dabbed at her lips again with her napkin. "I think, first of all, that the boys should have a basic language forum, examining their language, and the hidden implications of what they say and read every day. So much has come to light on this in the last few years, that a whole new field is opening up in such thought alone. They can help detect and redefine unfavorable terms as surely as anyone with formal training, once they realize what to look for. That is what is so exciting, the genuine discovery and effect that they can have." She poured herself half a cup more. "I think what St. Benedict needs is a more varied and current reading curriculum, as I mentioned. I am fully certified to teach and believe that once a more standard reading list is installed, I will have the time to teach a course or two myself, in feminine literature or women in church history. After all, I have all the plans for those classes already."

"That's very ambitious," I said. "They're not so used to women, you know, except the more traditional sisters here."

"Yes, isn't that just the point?"

I wasn't aware that it was.

"And the women they do see don't seem quite human, do they, in those out-moded habits? I suppose you still have penguin jokes?" She laughed. I answered with my laughter and arced eyebrows. "That's all right. We do have permission to standardize our dress. I plan on a big shopping spree with the sisters."

I was glad I hadn't eaten much. I wondered what time it was.

"But that's nothing to do with the boys." Oh no? I thought.

"Oh, don't worry, Father, I don't plan on turning things upside-down. But these little upgrades will make quite a difference. And you're welcome to sit in on any of these new courses any time."

"When do you think they will begin?"

"Not until next year. After all, we've only a couple months left until summer break, don't we? I'll just watch and get a feel for the place for now. But it is so lovely, and I'm very glad to be a part of all the excitement here. You know it's all the talk of the diocese of course."

"I'm sure."

"You must be thrilled."

"It's all pretty overwhelming."

"Yes, well. My, this has been ever so pleasant, but I think I really should be going. There are a thousand things to do."

"Of course." She rose and I followed. We shook hands again. "Glad you like it here. If you need anything at all . . . "

"Thank you. You really must get out in that sun. It's just lovely." She ducked her head into the hallway. "Thanks, Hilda!"

There was a large thump and some kind of convivial murmur from the depths. "Father, again, nice meeting you. Bye, now."

"Good-bye." With a twist of her skirt, she was gone. I folded up my newspaper. I knew what it was now, making her different. She was pretty.

✛

Good Friday was suffocation. How somber, how heavy the day was, the church wailingly open all day, the workers gone. The truly devoted streamed out their visits so that someone seemed to be in the church at all times. Profound, formal sadness hung in the air like stagnant drapes of smoke. The fast was observed throughout the staff. Then, at six o'clock, the service began. The altar servers proceeded me up the aisle in a long, slow, swinging line. The censure was a silver weight in my hands. I glanced at Tommy. I hadn't permitted him to serve. I knew this would be an emotional time for him and didn't know what form its effects would take.

He stared at the crucifix, the life-size Christ figure laid over the altar step that led to the sanctuary. This crucifix was painted, to be lifelike, with thick knobs of dry gathered paint bleeding over the ankles and wrists. The eyes bored upward, their focus lost in the tangle of thorns girding the brow. We read the passion. The play dialogue, really, is what it amounts to. One reader played Pilate, one Peter, and so on, and I read the lines of Christ. He was handed over to the soldiers, kept the night through, and in the morning, brought before Pilate and the people for judgment.

"What is his crime?" Pilate asked. "This man claims to be the King of the Jews. What would you have me do with your

King?"

The congregation now chants "Crucify Him! Crucify Him! Crucify Him!"

Every year, I found this eerie, the excitement growing in this tame group of people whom I knew, the horrid thrill of violence charging through them like a wave. I looked to Tom. He was pained, plainly, tears streaming down both his cheeks. He looked sad in the most desperate of ways, a tragic grief not befitting his young years. It was too large for him, the feeling, requiring more space than his small, frail form allowed. I saw the bones of his shoulders heave with this and somewhat of sickness, sure, and I missed a beat in the script as he faltered and clutched the pew.

The people chanted their lines on and on, their uniform cadence a weird surprise. "We have no King but Ceasar!"

Tom blinked and looked up and blinked again. I looked down at the crucifix lying across the step, a tremendously poorly done thing, and tried to refocus myself on the service. It was coming, the horrible moment.

"And so they crucified Him."

"Eloi, Eloi, why have you forsaken me?" I spoke the final words of Christ.

The silence that followed blackened the church with a bemoaning real and present, the creaks of five hundred kneelers biting and subsiding as the candles flickered on.

We rose without a word. The servers cleared the side altar cloths, the antependium, the frontal, the corporal, and I gathered the communion linens, the chalice veil, palla, and paten. The altar was stripped. The marble, always so beautiful, stood exposed in an obscenely vulnerable way, blank bands of alabaster and onyx standing helpless beneath the plain uncovered slabs. Everything seemed to be happening underwater, other beings unreachable, held at bay through the dense liquid, all swallowed whole. One by one, the people approached the large crucifix, knelt before it, and kissed its feet. I wiped the figure with cloth between each kiss. Once they passed through this way, they left the church.

A few remained. More would come throughout the night. Finally there would be Midnight Mass. Tom hadn't moved from his pew. I was worried about him. He hadn't kissed the cross, and this was extremely out of character for him. A half hour went by. Three persons still knelt toward the back. I knelt next to Tom in the front row. He wasn't moving, his eyes closed. I looked at his hands, the hands which knew their posture so well, the folding of prayer. My heart lurched—they were deep purple and grotesquely swollen. I sat. What was right? Should I respect his privacy, his prayer, or throw myself through this barrier, destroy his experience, and see whether there was danger? They grew positively black, and suddenly I reached for them, pulling them off the pew. The pull wrenched him, and his hands fell into my lap, staying together as a unit. His sleeve pulled, revealing thick leather strips crisscrossing the wrists, bound so tightly the skin swelled as if to burst through the gaps, his fingernails shrinking into the glutted cushion of flesh.

My heart. I grabbed my pocketknife from my black slacks and cut the strips. They lashed back with a snap, the rush of color surging Gothic horror too real to describe. The mere thought of it, the vision that stays with me even now, ever ready to spring to life as vividly as if it were happening now . . . a garish image.

I don't know how he got the straps tied. I didn't examine the knots afterward or the leather. I wrapped it up and put it in a cloth high in my closet. I never wanted to touch it again, be it as it was, touched by holiness.

Well, I questioned him the next day in confession, and he said that he had been commanded to distress himself thusly for the forgiveness of the sins of the parishioners. And what could I say to that?

Mother Christina, as she wished to be called, focused all of her energy on the school and breathed much excitement into the air around her.

"They are very minor things to change, Father, but in fact the impact is enormous. People have been reciting the same words for centuries, and each time enforces the idea of sexism and the oppression of women. I'm sure you'll agree.

"Our forefathers were obviously not all fathers. Perhaps a better term would be 'forerunners' or 'forebearers.' 'For the forgiveness of sins of all men' could be changed to simply 'all.' The songs sung to 'My brother' can rhythmically be replaced with 'neighbor.' There are so many changes that seem so slight, yet they can make such a difference."

As sure as she was that her enthusiasm would be shared by the young, unimpressioned boys, she was much surprised to find that more than a few had other views on the matter.

"But if we've never been aware of it being insulting, how could it be? It's all in the intent, after all." I watched silently from the back of a classroom. It happened to be a math class, but somehow the subject had come up. Again.

"It's so subliminal, the message that women are inferior. It's all a patriarchy, you see. You take it for granted, but it's there, all the while. That's just it; you aren't aware of it."

"But it sounds silly, all people instead of all men. Everyone knows that pertains to both men and women."

"It sounds odd because it is unfamiliar. There's another instance. You said 'both men and women.' Why not 'women and men?'"

"What's the difference?" They were very bold with her. She allowed it.

"I think it makes you more aware of it when you have to pause and sort out something like he/she on a page. Anyway, people get all caught up in these things and lose the whole value of what they're reading, or hearing."

"It only needs notice until it's ingrained. Then it will come naturally."

"He/she doesn't roll off the tongue." Laughter.

"Why do all notable women have to be noted as women?"

"What do you mean?"

"Women writers, women scientists, women producers, women leaders; you see it everywhere. Seems a waste of ink to me. We don't say Rembrant was a great man artist. It feels like a jab, a snag that catches you and says, 'Hey, this is a woman, and don't you forget it. You can never appreciate her fully if you are a man reading this article about her. Women are different."

"Women are different."

"Don't I know it. But that makes it seem like a whole different species, a whole different entity, rather than human."

"You have been conditioned."

"And you haven't?"

She was disturbed, after such discussions, but she took it on as a challenge, to make these boys see the light. A thoroughly Catholic trait, I thought. I left them on their own as much as possible. I knew I wasn't part of this new way, and Downtown knew it, too. I passed through now and then to reacquaint myself, and take in the nuances. The last time I was through, there was a display in the downstairs showcase of Great Women in the Church, period-dressed mannequins representing Mary, a variety of saints, St. Joan of Arc, St. Clare, St. Theresa the Little Flower. The pope who had turned out to be female beneath the robes was represented for a short time, until Downtown got wind of it and instructed it be removed. She was not considered an admirable figure of the Church. Mother Christina was stone and she was firey about her mission, and if nothing else, one had to be impressed with her perseverance. Frankly, for me, that impression was as palpable as the nothing else.

Keeping Tommy's public life private was something in itself, but not near so difficult as keeping his private life private was becoming. Hilda had such a close and fierce watch on him that I often had to tell her outright that I needed to talk to him alone in order to save his practices from her eyes, practices she probably wouldn't have understood. The fasting alone was giving her fits.

I came in very late one night from a meeting to find his door closed, but with the palest wavering of light leaking out underneath. The clues of candlelight. I was afraid to leave him alone in prayer for long lengths of time now, lest his excesses of penance overcome what was actually required of him. He only took penances now as dictated to him through the visions, and it was work to keep up with him. I opened the door. The sweet smell of sandalwood and frankincense entwined me like an embrace, lifting my senses and delighting me entirely. It was invisible near the door, but curling grey from two rapidly burning sticks on his dresser, placed on either side of a laminated rendering of Christ's Face and Sacred Heart. He knelt before it, half the side of the dresser, arms outstretched in the form of a cross. All seemed calm enough until I walked up alongside him. As my perspective shifted, I could make out a very thin line, reaching from a knob on the topmost drawer to his neck. Clear, shining, like water. Fishline. The paper-thin skin of his throat puffed up around it, swallowing it, his face swelling with the same discoloration as his neck. His eyes were slightly bulged. I shoved him forward immediately and pried at the string. It was fitted with a slipknot. Even as my shaking fingers picked it loose with maddening slowness, I was thinking that he must have intended just some deprivation and lost control. He had no idea how close he was to death. He fell into my arms, and I laid him on the bed, my entire body shaking, with emotions I could not name. I looked at the picture of the Sacred Heart on my way out. The eyes were still smiling, so kind and so calm.

✛

Tommy would graduate this year. Preparations were being made for the ceremony, new committees and new flowers. It was a relatively simple event. It took place in the church, lasted a couple hours, and was followed by a reception in the school gymnasium. The trusses were all erected, though, and the presence of scaffolding and dropcloths everywhere had people looking more to the gymnasium. I granted permission, and the entire ceremony was scheduled for the gym. Really, it did make sense, and wouldn't be difficult, only a little less atmospheric. But then, most of the boys had probably spent more time in the gym than in the church anyway.

It was May, and the boys were antsily moving through a rehearsal. I happened to be passing through, and sat down in the bleachers to watch.

"Hey, Father!" One caught me, and they all turned and waved. I waved back, and made a comic motion for them to carry on. They enjoyed it. The new Mother Superior stood at the head of their lines and formations, holding a clipboard on which she frequently noted things. The boys were quick to volunteer when asked to run. They were lively and attentive. She was a hit. Other sisters managed their individual classes, more or less standing on the sidelines and watching. They seemed such a world away from the nuns they had been just a few months ago; they all had hair and necks. I suppose we were one of the last to break out of the habit. Whether it was Mother Superior herself, or the relaxed pedestrian atmosphere, or graduation, or spring, the boys were boisterous and active. I looked around for Tommy but couldn't find him. The boys looked different—yes—they were wearing hats! And some wore bandanas and pins apart from the uniform. What a smudge of surprise this place was anymore. No, he wasn't here to be found. I watched a little while and walked on.

His dorm room was empty. I had an idea of where he was now. The spring sun warmed me as I crossed over to the church, doors open, letting out the sounds of drills and hammers, and a sporadic voice here and there. Such a big team they had working on this! The windows were nearing completion, the wiring and whatnot being revamped before and as the inner walls began to appear. They had scrupulously kept as sectional as possible with the work, so that they could be worked around, but there was no ignoring their presence even when they had long gone home. Now, as I looked around, I could see that this was no place for even the most concentrated mediation, and wandered down the aisle, wondering where Tom could be. I felt myself grimace as worker after worker passed in front of the tabernacle without so much as a nod. In fact, old law is that such workers are allowed to pass to and fro like that, so long as they genuflect at the beginning and the end of their workday. But had they? I had my doubts. The sacristy held no one outside of passing workers, and I moved to leave. Then, toward the side doors, I paused. Was it locked? I tried the door. No, the confessional was open. The door opened to the vision of a cowlicked silhouette behind the daytime grate. His head was bowed and didn't jar at all when I entered. I closed the door behind me and sat, not making any sound. A while passed thus, the only sounds being those of the muffled construction. Then he spoke.

"He came to me last night. He was so beautiful, so utterly and unspeakably beautiful. His long hair flowed out with the radiance from His face and His eyes." His voice was full of peace, an unbroken line of calm, perhaps the only thing that was calm around here. I didn't bother about the rehearsal. He was where he should be. I knew that. I listened to him describe the beauty of the vision, the careful and consistent image of Christ that he had always reported and the quiet murmur of joy that took him further and further away from this world.

✝

The gymnasium held about a thousand visitors in all, piled up in the bleachers, stacked with their purses and cameras behind rails wreathed in crepe paper and tissue flowers. White hair, black hair, red, yellow, infinite shades of brown, bald heads, hatted heads, they all stayed as much put as possible, wavering and leafing through programs and boxes of cough drops when the still standing was too much.

The choir had sung a string of songs for the last forty minutes as people filed in, and now began the opening. For a change, I stood as others entered in a procession, two straight lines of suits draped in thin navy blue robes. Such somber faces they were, as if this morning the boys had woken up mature and settled adults in the world. The seats all finally filled, I began the opening prayer. Songs, tributes, and trustees passed between the home and visitor courts, camera bulbs flashing despite being forbidden, camcorders shining their little red lights, until one by one, the boys came to me, their names being read into the microphone by the Mother Superior Christina, and shook my hand as I handed them their coveted vinyl-covered folios. I remembered their faces five years back, as they each approached me with such formality on Confirmation. Some I had even handed their First Communion wafer. Now they were larger and taller, with shadows of facial hair or even a full mustache. The last diploma was granted, and we all retired for a moment of quiet reflection, the choir playing a low instrumental with a thoughtful flute line. The wave had crested now, and the whole gymnasium breathed with a quieted air, hands still and folded into laps.

A form rose from the third row and came toward the platform. Mother Christina glanced at me sharply and tightened. This was not in the program. It kept coming, a slow sure approach. It was Tommy. He stopped before the step, directly in front of the crucifix, placed there just for the ceremony between an American and the state flag, and he knelt down on the wooden floor, hands folded before him in prayer. The tension had hit in the choir, and in the boys; the visitors waited to see what this part of the program was. I started to rise, and he spoke, his voice so striking and compelling that I was frozen to my chair.

"This our Lord says to us: that we have a duty unto Him, and He is here in our midst. Yes, Lord. Yes, Lord. He stands there, surrounded by light, before the doorway to heaven. All who wish to enter must pass through Him." In the bleachers, his mother had buried her face in her husband's shoulder. He sat very tall and drawn. Mother Christina looked around and rose, bending to Tommy's ear and touching his shoulder. Her movement had no effect; she used some pressure, but his body did not yield. I gathered my senses and went to them. Tommy stared up at a space before the crucifix, eyes glazed and unblinking.

"Tom," I spoke lightly. "Tom, you must get up." I tried in vain to move him, yet I knew full well that it would be impossible at this point. He was in a state, and nothing was going to speed it. Murmurs started now, as people realized that something was going on. Mother looked at me.

"Can't you lift him?" She asked.

"No. He's as good as rooted there."

"Well, for pity's sake . . ."

Tommy spoke again, filling the gymnasium with the authority of his young timber.

"He tells me to explain that He is there, with arms outstretched, waiting. I must tell you this because He has not revealed this to all."

The boys were really agitated now.

"Marc, come here." Mother was really flustered now. "Just get him up."

Marc was there in an instant, and for all his linebacker strength, there was no way he was going to get him up either.

Two more boys volunteered themselves, to no avail. Oblivious, cement, Tom raised his voice in full command.

"He is there! Look! The faithful: See! His wounds are poured through with light, red and white, His holy crown is jeweled mixture of thorn and gold. Behold your Savior!"

People were standing now, and coming to the lower bleachers for a closer look. The boys were speaking in audible tones, and more were coming to try and disengage him.

"What's going on down there?" Someone yelled.

"A vision! He's having a vision!"

"Sacrilegious stuntman!" How instantly vocal they were, how quickly triggered into excitement. This could turn into disaster in an eyeblink. They tried desperately to lift him, to jar him, anything, while the floor filled with people from the bleachers. I sank as the local doctor and three off-duty policemen made haste down the aisle. They were ten feet away, then five, he couldn't be moved, no way, the world about to forever alter as their suited sleeves reached for his transfixed form, the shine of a ruby ring on one hairy hand, and then—

Unbelievable. A huge beam crashed through the ceiling, with a white smash of plaster and lights, screams tearing through with the wild confusion of people running on instinct, without plan, tripping and knocking into one another. The choir escaped as lights exploded and shattered onto the floor, the sledge of the crash falling directly onto the platform, where I had been a moment ago. About ten feet of the beam hung through the hole. Light broke through, flashing off the cloud of dust swirling up and filling the space, and as suddenly as it blinded with white, it closed over, like the drawing of a lid, and blinded with blackness. The entire gym was plunged into utter darkness, the screams flying infectiously, Pandemonium now unseen. I touched him on the face. He was frozen and stone cold. Two minutes it was, two minutes with the stretch of eternity, and God only knows what people were doing in their blind terror. Then the light began again. Silence fell over the whole room as it edged in, a growing shaft falling through the opening, spilling over the edge of the beam, reaching the floor, the shapes of fallen ceiling pieces and roofing, my chair knocked over, the flags lying on the rubble, but the crucifix standing tall. Powder of white reflected from it like snow or some eerie emanation, and the light expanded, stretching across the platform to where the choir had been, over the music stands, the deserted piano. It filled the rest of the room with half-light, as the electric was gone, and showed a disjointed and scattered mob of people, chairs awry, programs everywhere, all faces riveted and staring at the opening. I looked down. Tom had given way and was a limp puddle on the floor. Without thinking, I picked him up as fast as I could and made for the emergency exit behind the crucifix which covered the locker room entrance. The voice of Mother Christina was already calling out for the attention of the crowd. Before anyone had a chance to act, we were gone across the yard, in a mad dash for the rectory. Hilda was standing in the backyard, looking at the monstrous beam perched between the church and the school roofs. She made for the door immediately and held it open wide as I raced inside with Tommy.

I laid him down on my bed and closed the door behind me. Hilda waited for me to speak. We went into the kitchen.

"I'll call the hospital. There may be people hurt. And I'll call the construction people. Don't let anyone in but Tom's parents or staff." She closed the doors, saw that I was in a turn, and gave me the numbers to dial. As I was on the phone, we heard sirens. It was, after all, a central part of town, and there were bound to be people with beepers and such in the crowd. The blare of fire engines pulled in invasively, and police sirens. There were a thousand knocks at the doors. Hilda let police in through the front.

"A beam fell through from the church roof; it's being worked on. I don't know just what happened. There may be people hurt; there was a lot of confusion."

"I'm sure. That and the eclipse."

"What?"

"Oh yeah," he was scribbling on a clipboard. "Didn't you guys notice? We just had an eclipse."

"Lord God in heaven" I said. He looked at me.

"Yea, well, we'll get everything in order. They're straightening out the panic now. Is there anything the crowd has to stay for?"

"No, not at all. It's over."

He unhitched a walkie-talkie from his belt and broke into the scratches it was sounding. "Hey, how you doing?"

A voice came back quite strong. "All right, a lot of confusion. A lot of folks cleared out already."

"Well, get them moving. It's over."

"Over."

"Over."

He replaced the device. "I've got men on the parking lot. We'll have it cleared out in about fifteen minutes, twenty at the most. Looks pretty good, just a lot of shake-up. You and I can just stay here and fill out the report, if you would."

"Certainly."

Hilda stepped in. "I'll put on some tea."

✠

It was at least two hours before everyone had gone, forms had been filled out, and other matters taken care of. Somehow the news had become involved and had made off again with urgency. I knew that when I could think about it, I would know this spelled trouble. The injuries were very minor. Paramedics kept saying we were very lucky, though they did set a broken arm and treated a lot of bumps and bruises. Parents wanted answers; everyone wanted them; however, the police were remarkably good at keeping them at bay and finally getting them to leave. Electricians and various repairmen were on the spot at the end of the hour though I was sure that nothing

102

would get done tonight. In fact, the holes in the school and in the church roofs did get covered with plastic, and the entire area was marked off. Fortunately in the immediate future, traffic would be reduced with school over with now. It was quite dark by the time everyone left, and only Tommy's parents remained. Hilda had been hosting them in a back room, settling them into large stuffed chairs and lighting the fireplace, I noticed, for purely therapeutic reasons as it was June. I smiled. It was thoughtful of her.

I had been hauled out for questioning. Hilda now made sure I had a full cup of tea before I went into the waiting room, to face the inquisitors I feared in all of this.

Hilda spoke. "Now, Father, they're all quieted down, just a bit tense, is all. They know Tom is all right, and they've seen him. He's still asleep. They didn't think he needed to see a doctor; they wanted to wait and talk to you first. They just want to know that he's o.k."

I sighed. "Thank you. You can stay around if you want."

"No, I'll be in and out. Now Father, he's graduated. And they will be thinking that he's going home tonight. But I really would suggest that he stay here for a while."

I looked at her. Her gaze was steady. "There's going to be a lot of excitement about him, probably more than any person needs at their house, and we've got plenty of room here. I don't see why he needs to rush home right now if you all are sure he isn't going to a hospital."

I nodded. My tea was steaming, and Hilda followed me with the ceramic pot into the room. It wasn't too hot with the fire; in fact, it was quite pleasant and finally quiet. Their faces weren't quiet, but they were. They sat very close to one another on one side of a long couch, the father sitting very conservatively, in his gawky way, and the mother with both hands wrapped around her mug. Hilda refilled it, taking care to use enough time for me to settle into the armchair across from them, at an angle, another little thing for which I was so grateful, in my numb blundering, or so it felt.

"Hello. How are the two of you?"

She spoke first. "Well, we're concerned, Father. How is Tommy? What happened out there?"

I organized my thoughts. "Tommy's fine. He's asleep right now as Hilda told you."

She looked to her husband. He cleared his throat. "Father, what was it that happened to him out there?"

This was it. Whatever happened from here on out, this was it. "Tom had a vision."

They were silent. They didn't register surprise or any abrupt reaction. They just kept looking at me and were silent.

"Tommy has visions, you know. He always has. I can't talk to you in detail about all of it, because what we discuss, we discuss in the confidence of confession." I took a breath. "But I believe him."

His father disengaged their lapse. "You know, you saw the records. The psychiatrist thought he has delusions, as did the priest in Minnesota -"

"I know. I know all that. He was very young when all of that took place. I've been his confessor for almost four years now, and I believe him."

"Well, then, the ceiling, the eclipse, all of that . . . "Her voice was strained and seemed very tired, the kind of tired that isn't born in a day. "Was it, a miracle, Father?" The tone wavered between neutrality and troubledness.

"I don't know about all of that. I won't say that it was or that it had anything to do with his vision, but then, who am I to say that it wasn't? I'm just a man." This did startle them a bit. Perhaps I shouldn't have said it. With it went a tiny bit of authority.

He leaned in. "But this is what everyone is going to want to know. What do we tell them? What do we say?"

"Say what you believe. Or don't tell anyone anything at all; you are under no obligation to answer anybody's questions.

Or tell them that you are waiting for the final analysis of the architects and the astronomers and the Church. That's what we're waiting for. Until then, who can say anything for sure?"

This seemed to subdue them with the effect that logic can have, and I seized the moment. "There will be a lot of confusion for a while. The press, the public, thrill-seekers, and the unstable, they're all going to be hounding Tom, to be frank with you." They were listening. "He is of legal age now, no longer a child. What I propose is this: why don't you leave Tom here, in our care, for a while? If he wants to stay, of course. We won't charge anything. It will be safe and relatively quiet for him to wait out some of the fuss here. But it is bound to be crazy for a while, no telling how long."

They looked at each other. I was prepared to step out while they conferenced, but they seemed to have instant agreement. They started to speak at the same time twice, and then she yielded.

"That would be fine, Father. That would be just fine, and we appreciate how generous an offer it is. It's a huge offer, and we'll be more than happy to help you or pay you whatever you think feasible -"

I waved this away. "No, not at all. He's no trouble. I do think it will be easier for him, and for you, and for St. Benedict's, too, to do it this way." Hilda appeared in the doorway. "Hilda will show you where he will stay, and whatever details need be. I am glad to see that you two are so level-headed about all of this, strange as it is, and I will be glad to help however I can." We were shaking hands animatedly, all of us, with a mixture of relief and resignation. Hilda came in and began clearing the tea things. I moved toward the door, the feeling of "what happens next?" in the air. Hilda straightened.

"Father, you're needed in the back. Now, can I show you two around?"

We exchanged good-byes, and I went off to my room. Tommy had been esconced to, I presumed, a guest room. I wandered around my sitting room, pouring myself a Scotch and memorizing how the books lined up in my bookcase, my mind too tired to think. I sat in my black leather armchair, pushed it back so that the footrest rose under my feet, and closed my eyes. All I needed was some music. I got up and put in Cavaleria Rusticana, Mascagni, and then sank back down into the chair, allowing the music to fill in my limbs and my throbbing head, taking the place of a hundred scattered voices and visages. All there was was the music, pure and unearthly in its perfection, each note a masterstroke. Intermezzo. Thank God.

✛

Hilda came through sometime very late. I had been sleeping on the chair.

"Hello, there, Father. Brought you a nightcap."

"Wonderful." I looked and saw that her nightcap was hot tea. That's all right. In fact, it seemed just the thing. She poured us both a cup and settled into another chair. We tended our tea for a long, quiet time, the stillness of the closed rectory deepened by the absorbing silence of the night. Chamomile, it was, with some blend of herbs that gave a mellow, soothing flavor to an otherwise empty-tasting tea. I sipped it gratefully.

"Well, this is the last night we'll have with the world intact," she said at length.

Intact. That was a curious choice of words. "You think it's never going to be the same again?" I didn't look up from my tea. It was such an engaging caramel color, swallowing up light and shape.

"No. No, I don't think so, Father. And this is going to take a long time to die down."

"Should we let anyone see Tommy?"

"Well now, let's see. He's going to be tired. He wasn't that well to begin with. Will he remember what happened?"

I thought. "I don't know. I think so."

"They'll ask him over and over, hundreds of times, maybe, and they won't all like what he'll say. Are you prepared to defend him?"

This all seemed a huge thing to think about. Well, it was, and unfortunately, there wouldn't be any time to "sleep on it." No amount of ignoring it would stave it away. She was right to have me sorting out my thoughts now.

"I can tell them the same things I told his parents, but that's about all. I really don't have all the answers. And the trouble is, my opinion can't count. Not really. I shouldn't say anything until the Church makes its decision on the matter. That could take years, in all probability, beyond your and my lifetimes. Beyond Tommy's. No, I shouldn't say anything."

"You're saying shouldn't. Makes me think you know that you will."

She knew me too well. I sighed. "I suppose you're right. But that's not what I should do. I should say something political and vague and gloss over it until an official decision comes down."

We were quiet again. I knew she was thinking that what I had just said was pointless. She knew where things stood better than I, and as they pertained to me! "I guess we can ask him what he wants. He probably knows the right thing to do anyway."

"Does he?"

"Well, no. He won't have any hold on what this means, what it is doing, what it will continue to do. He won't have any idea."

"Then you have to make the decision for him."

I sipped. "He can't be completely absent. The public won't have it, and we could be asking for trouble. Perhaps what he should do is issue one statement, to whoever will count the most and it can be distributed to everyone else. Yes, that's it. But who is that, I wonder? The largest news station, I guess. We won't have long to wait for a syndicated report. I guarantee it. So that's what we'll do. What do you think?"

"Sounds sensible, Father. He should be kept on the sidelines as long as possible."

"Yes, I think that is the thing to do."

She poured me more tea.

"Thank you. . . What do you think, Hilda?"

We had never discussed it. It was a respectfully untouched issue. She poured herself some more. "The Lord works in strange ways. I can't understand them. He's a holy boy, that's sure. He's sickly, and he needs looking after in plenty of ways, that's sure too."

"But do you believe in him?" In fact, I'd never asked that of anyone. Right now, I needed to know from her, whatever her answer was. She smiled.

"Doesn't matter, Father. I'm just here to help things go smoothly; that's all. Not my place to be passing judgments."

I'd thought at first that she was hiding her answer, reluctance borne of disagreement perhaps. Now I realized that she really had told me all there was to her opinion. How pleasant that must be, not to have to make a decision about everything, to just co-exist with mysteries and leave the dither to others. Makes sense. I couldn't do it.

"I believe in him, Hilda. But I'm not an hysteric about it. Whether or not all the surrounding business has to do with him, I really don't know, but I believe in him. I don't see why it couldn't be connected. A lot of coincidences, all of that to be happening at once. But I guess we'll have to wait and see."

"Fair enough. Tomorrow morning it will start, and you'll need all the training you got from the renovation hoopla. I'll make you a heaping breakfast that'll really pack it on your ribs, and the same with dinner, whenever that'll be. Don't worry about any of that. Tommy will get plenty more of the same. Meantime, you've got a big day head of you; so I suggest you get yourself off to bed. Much better for the back than that kinked-up chair."

I sat up. She took my cup from my hand. "Thank you, Hilda. Thanks a lot. I mean it, not just for this, but for . . . everything . . . "

She was stacking the tea tray. "That's just fine. Now get yourself to bed."

"Okay." I got up slowly, and shuffled off down the hall.

✠

Yes, it was mayhem. It began at 6:30, with phone calls from the diocese. The construction crew hauled in at 8:00.

"Jesus Christ! Will you look at that!" Rough but capable, the foreman looked at me. "I knew it was bad, but this is crazy. You say there was nothing; it just slid in?"

"That's right. It was completely quiet around here. Just the ceremony."

He whistled. "Well, you see here, what happened is more than an ordinary accident. It's plain bizarre." He raised his eyebrows with an incredulous laugh that wouldn't stop until I joined him.

"There should have been no way that beam could have given way like that. You see, we had it up there for the suspended ceiling. It was going to be lowered from the scaffolding today. And it fell at just such an angle, that . . . Jesus. It was secure; it was absolutely secure. I would take responsibility if I had the slightest inclination that it was because of my boys. But you see, it wasn't. I checked that beam myself before we closed shop."

It had been suspended on a scaffold between the church and the school, which was considerably taller than the school building, which was newer, and had been built quite close to the church. They had opened up a space in the roof that was deteriorating anyway and causing some electric problems, and the space provided a perfect opening to lower the suspension beams and chains through, unconventional a method as it was. With a crane, it was entirely practical, and of course, budget meant nothing to the church. They had been reporting all along that it had all been going very well.

"It just doesn't add up. You see what I'm saying?"

I nodded.

"I mean, if it had been a storm, or something, then maybe, but just to up and fly like that, you see?'

"Yes, I do. Well, can you fix it?"

"Can we? Oh, sure. No problem. I'll get another crew on the school right away. But this brings up another thing, Father. If we can get that gym patched up quickly, how feasible is it for you to hold Mass there? I mean, I wouldn't care, and I know they told you we could work it so that you didn't have to move, but really, I think you can see that it's impossible. We haven't even started tearing up the sacristy floor yet. That's coming up."

"Mmhm."

He gave a little laugh. "Really, I don't know why they even told you that. It's not going to be possible to keep it going there, it really isn't. You know what a pain it is to hold it now, with the ceiling work going on."

I nodded. "Yes, I know."

"You see?"

"Yes, I see." I did. I'd known it for quite some time. We just didn't have a chapel. Never had need for one up till now. Anyway, the thought had occurred to me during their rehearsal one day. It would be feasible. Least of our worries soon, I should think. I got whisked away by some local reporters and laid out arrangements later in the day for the essential items of the church to be hauled over to the school. Until the gym was in order, which shouldn't take too long, we could use the auditorium. I felt like a Scotch at noon.

But noon was lunch with Hilda and Tommy, and I cleared away the spot with great determination to enjoy it. The small back kitchen was cosy and quiet, while on the other side of the rectory, phones were ringing off the hook and typists were banging away. We had a lovely pot roast and potatoes, with a green salad and fontinella cheese. I was so relieved to see that Tom wasn't fasting at the moment, and we all managed to do Hilda's great spread justice with our appetites. We talked very little, and then about nothing at all, and in fact, I brought out the paper. It was from morning, but I hadn't gotten to it yet. The headline was the untimely eclipse, the second piece international, but the bottom of the page was a hit on the jaw.

BENEDICT MIRACLE OR MAYHEM?

Yesterday evening found the graduates of St. Benedict High School looking toward their futures with a new wonderment. The alleged vision of graduating senior Thomas Peterson, son of Lawrence and Sherri Peterson, was immediately followed by an unexplainable construction catastrophe and the untimely eclipse of the sun for ninety-eight seconds.

The Church, which is currently undergoing renovation, was being prepared for a new drop ceiling, a beam of which perched atop scaffolding between the two buildings. As Peterson cried out that he saw an apparition of Jesus Christ standing in front of the crucifix at the front of the gymnasium, the beam unaccountably slipped from its place and crashed through the ceiling of the gym, destroying several light fixtures, reports say. Immediately following this event, the eclipse occurred. The ensuing panic resulted in one broken arm and numerous topical treatments, many of resulting from shock and fright.

"It was really crazy," said trustee Jonathan Beumont. "We didn't know what was going on."

School principal and Mother Superior Christina Rhodes took charge of the situation. "We don't know what happened out there. We can't say anything at this time. We're just grateful that not many were hurt."

Peterson was unavailable for comment, as was the pastor of St. Benedict Church, Reverend Mulcarthy. Mulcarthy carried the boy to the church rectory, reports say.

I hastily folded the paper and put it down. Tommy appeared unaware of anything. Hilda gave me a subtly sympathetic look. I reached for more potatoes.

☩

"What is this? What is going on?"

The mahogany desk gleamed between us. I hadn't sat before the Bishop in years.

"Just what you already know. The paper got it right. It all happened within seconds while he was having this vision."

"Our telephones have been ringing nonstop with this business. I'm sure yours have. I want the whole story. Who is this boy? What is this business about visions?"

I had hoped for a calmer atmosphere, but there we were. I had brought Tom's file, and showed it to him now, explaining as clearly as I could about his mysticism, without breaking the confidence. The whole talk lasted about an hour and a half, until, I suppose, he had satisfied himself that anything else would only be repetition. He ate up the information like a machine, digesting it as quickly and thoroughly as possible.

"This is not bizarre," he said. "At the best, he is an unfortunate anachronism. At the worst, he is an hysteric. You have some stock in him, for whatever reason." He pushed his chair back and looked straight ahead. "The sensation this has caused is huge. There will be a full investigation, of Thomas Peterson, of the visions, and of your church construction." He looked at me. "Say nothing of your personal feelings about any of this. Inform the public that the investigation has been instituted. I will have two letters drafted and faxed by this evening: one for your parish, and one for the press release."

We left it at that. He was right about the anachronism bit. Tom would have been completely acceptable in the church some one, two, or five hundred years ago, but this was the twentieth century, and he didn't fit.

Catholics from the nineteenth century had visions; they feared hell with a terror; they fasted and inflicted themselves. Hell, in medieval times, it was a regular practice for entire communities to move through the streets, flagellating themselves for their sins. They wore hair shirts—undershirts of sharp and scratchy fiber, worn to induce a state of perpetual irritation. The mortification, the whole matter of one's faith was a personal thing, regulated by one's confessor. It was no one else's business. These people were not regarded as anything extreme (I can't say that with entire truth, of course. But the general view of such practices fell into a completely different sensitivity of beliefs and self-awareness that people were growing cold to today); rather, this was all quite common. Anyway, he was extraordinary in real physical phenomena: the Friday fevers, the never-discussed levitation (?), the states that he entered into in his visions—the stone coldness, like death. I was afraid of discussing this too extensively with the Bishop for fear that Tommy would become some medical guinea pig, but in my secret beliefs, I knew that in these moments, Tommy in fact had no pulse at all. And he wasn't the first mystic in the history of the Church with whom that was the case. The trouble was that he didn't fall into the category of the mediocre visionary or the overzealous follower. Tom was the quintessential saint extraordinaire, and it was inevitable that as such would suffer at the hands of the mad, blundering world.

✠

It didn't die down. By the time the roof was repaired in the gym, five hundred people on an average were showing up there for each Sunday Mass, where Mass was held instead of the church. It was absurd: people filled the floor, stacked in the bleachers, and stood along the walls. They wanted to see the spot, the very spot of the apparition. As it was yet unverified, the spot could not be marked in any way, and so the same questions went on and on; where was it? Wnd where was the boy? Where was the beam? Those outside the parish were much more liable to give the vision credence than those who actually belonged to St. Benedict. It was a very difficult summer, with all the attention that should have gone into other matters being burned up by miracle-seekers and protesters.

The press was relentless. The entire incident had attracted national and even some international coverage, including the tabloids, with all of their worthlessness and ill-repute. They ate it up. This was one story that needed no embellishment. I couldn't understand why it persisted. The eclipse, granted, had not been logical, but there had been a scientific explanation for the aberration. The question remained of course: what had caused the aberration? The same with the beam. The same with it all. It filled some mixture of human needs, I supposed, whatever makes such things an obsession. There it was, and there was nothing anybody could do to quiet it down.

Only Tommy remained unchanged. Guarding him was a full-time job. Everyone wanted Tommy, reporters, talk shows, psychiatrists, lunatics, the ill, the crippled, all with their own individual needs and curiosities, which invariably had nothing to do with Tommy. Perhaps keeping him a secret was feeding into the mystique of it all and making it worse. I don't know. But somehow, the alternative of letting him be eaten up by this swamp of rats seemed unthinkable. Hilda honestly agreed on this point and looked after him like a mother lion her young.

He talked to me often, about his inner life of visions and visitations. He wanted to know if he had caused any harm with all the excitement. I told him no. He was concerned about being a nuisance to Hilda and to me and to his parents, whom he had never talked about much. Hilda kept him sensibly busy with tasks about the place, things like lists and addresses and dishes and most especially reading. She was very strong on this point of reading, though she never brought it up to me. She gave him the classics that had nothing to do with religion. I didn't know whether it was a diversion, a personal conviction about child-rearing, or a wish to know these books that spurred her to persist; I don't think she'd read them herself. She didn't seem the literary type, but then how was I to know? I would pass him in the day sitting by a window with a copy of Dickens or Bronte on his lap. Lots of poetry, Emerson and Coleridge. And for every piece he read, she required him to make a thorough entry into a reading journal. It was his duty while he lived here, and it seemed to suit him perfectly. I was glad to see this odd arrangement take form between them, and it really made me gain respect for Hilda, in a whole new way. I didn't feel it was my province to inquire, so I'll never know the privacies of their hardback, leather-bound symbiosis, but it was a comforting thing to witness.

The leaves began their ritual turning, the rich theatre of the natural lands translating into occasional spirals of loose brown husks rising from the pavements in the city. Downtown sent me two assistant priests for the holiday, though it looked as if they were a bit more permanent than that. That was all right; I didn't mind. I was getting very tired. They were both younger than me and fresh to the fanfare; it had more than lost its novelty for me. I reinstated the old fixed schedule, since there were no limitations with the gym.

The gymnasium still had to accommodate the athletic activities, of course, so each week involved a transitioning of rowed chairs and moveable altar pieces with tennis shoes and rubber balls. School proceeded with all the normal smooths and snags of the start of the year. The new class came with their clowns and their brains and their overall flavor of fear and curiosity. It was going on.

✠

And the world wanted Tommy. They demanded him. The din rose to a roar as a rumor unleashed that he was being held prisoner, captively rattling off streams of otherwordly messages. In fact, he was doing that; he always had. But the new sense of urgency that the public gave it somehow cheapened rather than enhanced it.

⊹

I drove again, stealing away each Friday in October for the evening, no matter what was happening. I didn't even tell Hilda where I was. No plan, no course, just blessedly mindless meandering as far from the city as I could manage. I went to the cemetery, I went to the woods, I went to my hometown, believe it or not. I wanted both a void of all the madness that was always there now and something of enough fortissimo to distract me from it. But nothing could. If I saw a magazine, it was there. If I saw a church, it was there. If I saw a young, overly-thin blonde boy with a cowlick, he was there. The cacophony of it all never left; it was like air, the tragedy of it all woven into the molecules of oxygen and carbon dioxide, clinging with the fatality of nitrogen in a crowded orbit.

I remember it all now, so clearly. I was driving on All Saints' Eve, through the earliest dim of twilight. One of the other priests was saying Mass, for which I was grateful. The endless parade of costumes through the rural streets continued at very turn. Capes swept the dust of times past into the here and now, altering reality. Ironically euphoric jack o'lanterns grinned jagged and crooked teeth through the light of candles, flickering unevenly with the chilling breeze. Streams of shining black hair, leering white faces, claws and wings. Halloween, Allhallows eve, the night the Pagans and Druids had called Samhain long before Christianity had come into being, when the veils are the thinnest between the two worlds, and the dead pass freely to intermingle with the living. Catholics of old dressed to emulate and honor a saint on All Saints' Day, November 1, when the Church honors all saints, both canonized and beatified. Later people masqueraded as any hero and finally as creatures of foreboding to ward off evil spirits, in the vein of totem poles and gargoyles. The belief began that demons took offerings of food to appease their wrath and haunting, which translated into trick or treating. Now there were no rules, and no perameters of expectation to fall within. A low dwarf darted in front of my car in a flash. I slammed on the breaks. It stared at me for a moment, hideous wrinkles of leathery myth crinkling round its sardonic glare. It ran on. Sounds, sounds of moans and wails, and creaking doors, filled the night, eeking and thundering from monstrously towering speakers in darkened houses, and some from live beings. They waddled, they wavered, lots led by bigger hands, a glistening pink fairy with the netted wings of a dragonfly, a horned garish red figure, with innocent white face peering from beneath the hood. Quick black phantoms snaked through the night, faster and more taunting, floating with the glide of wheels under their flowing black crepe. Where there was no sound, the silence was more horrible, that huge crackling silence of tension. It smothered the night like a blanket, inescapable feeling of anticipation, and danger, as infiltrating and unstoppable as a smell.

I arrived back at St. Benedict's in the heart of the night, parking my car in the garage, locking it securely. I didn't go into the rectory, but passed round the side of it to the church. The key turned with furtive falls of clinks and clamps. It was black.

I knelt in the closed and darkened church, looking for all of its transitioning like a battlefield of gorgeous ruins from the Vatican. The dome was obscured with the thin but complete foundation for the dropped ceiling, the windows intact. The graceful statues and golden figures laid ajar in haphazard placing, anywhere that they could be secure enough and decidedly out-of-the-way. Two gilded angels knelt in the gut where front pews had been, one facing the exit door, one on its side. Great jagged slabs of marble rised up along their faultlines, rearing toward the sky and trying vainly to sink into the earth. The crucifix laid on a bare patch of sanctuary floor, the body removed, but the wooden cross remaining. The elegant dome proscenium no longer arched protectively over its emaciated marble form. Instead, exposed drywall seared past the INRI, and strips of torn velvet wallpaper hung in limp exposure of the naked wall underneath. Old wood stood out foreignly where tapestry had gleamed.

I took the sanctuary candle out from the sacristy and stood it in front of the siege, on the bare, whitely dusty place where the communion rail had one stood. It stood upright, its tall Gothic ironwork holder, with more detail than all of these new windows combined, and touched the smooth, perfect red glass column of its holder. I lit the blackened wick, its traces of beeswax flaring up and then becoming calm with the stillness of the single flame in a draftless room. I stood over it for a long while, the flame too bright to stare at, but beckoning all the more, the tiny burn of blue at its bottom. It ate oxygen, it gave back heat, and light, and it had presence in the Church before any one person or work of art, no matter how elaborate. It was respected, finally, perhaps the only thing that could be respected by every person all at once, regardless of his beliefs or experiences. Fire was an entity unto itself, the simple enigma that floated with effortless power and beauty.

I knelt in one of the still-standing pews farther back, knelt and fixed my stare on the red glow. Gradually, I became keenly aware of a presence in the Church, behind me. Surely, I would have heard someone else come in; the doors were all shut and locked. It was there, an unearthly feel, not necessarily disquieting, as it was not the sensation of being watched, but an almost tangible presence in the darkness. I turned. Tommy knelt in the very back of the Church,   at the foot of the main aisle, which was now without carpet. He knelt on the cement floor, which must have been hard on his knees, I kept thinking, *that floor must be hard on your knees*, and his eyes were far, far away, fixed but likely unseeing, straight ahead. I eased back into the pew and winced at the creak of the wood in the silence. He was there. I was glad. I closed my eyes. Then I heard the thud.

I ran back. He had collapsed somehow onto his side, thank God not his face, and was breathing quite hard. His body was soft and limp, not stiff, so I didn't think it was one of his raptures. Perhaps one had just passed. I waited beside him for a long time, until his breathing became not so labored, but curiously intense. He looked at me.

"Father, you must help this servant of the Lord."

His voice was his but not his, with a command of authority such as it had possessed during the graduation vision. I sat next to him.

"Whatever I can do."

He stretched his face upward, eyes cast toward the sky. "The Lord is my shepard!" He cried. His voice was suddenly wild and passionate, with the high pitch of crisis. He breathed very fast, now, as if he couldn't get enough air for his activity, the thin bones of his throat straining through his skin. He was seeing something, something vivid and real, something so immense that even I glanced up to see what it was. He was sweating, his mouth expressively closing and opening wide, in awe and fear and climactic ecstasy. His eyes, so wide they might snap, with such goodness that I felt my stomach pull in answer to the emotion, were pools of full dilation. His hair fell back away from his face, the ends of it lost in the framing darkness. He was engulfed with the most absolute passion I have ever seen in any human being, and I have seen mothers wailing over their dead sons and lovers torn apart forever, children being brought into the world and the ecstasy of both woman and man in my bed, long ago. Nothing, no matter how extreme, could approach the consummation in his eyes. I was overwhelmed and could do nothing but look at him.

"Father!" it was a whisper of unutterable power. "Father, you must help me!"

"What, my son? What can I do?"

He turned his wild eyes on me and whispered with restrained precision, "You must help me finish. I cannot do it myself." He held out his hands. They were covered in blood, flowing from purpled holes in the wrists. Cartilage was pushed through the tops of his forearms. It made me sick.

"Tommy!" I cried.

His voice was a furnace of gentle caress. "Father, it is all right. The Lord has given to me his suffering, and I hasten to His call. He has wished it to be so." How pale he was, I noticed. More than usual. But his face blazed with this otherworldly fire. "He has given me to you, tonight, to meet out His Will. He will take me, now, Father, His Arms are open wide."

I was crying now, the tears blurring my view. He seemed to be glowing with light all over and through his clothes. He touched me on the cheek, lifting my face toward him.

"Do not weep, Father. This is my greatest moment. I am to be with Him, all eternity in His Breast. He has spoken that you must help me now, Father, for I cannot complete this myself."

He walked with perfect ease, despite the flow from his feet, toward the altar. His hands hung at his sides. A line of white light surrounded his entire form, and shone through the wounds in his wrists and his feet.

"Come, Father. Follow the Will of our Lord."

I got up, staggering in my grief, and forced myself to follow him. He was on the altar now, the spot cleared of marble, where the wood cross lay. He laid down over it, stretching out his arms and legs, his feet fitting perfectly onto the wedge to support them, his head at the top. He was bliss and kindness and angst all at once, the light growing and hurting my eyes.

"Come, Father. You are my child. I love you. Do as you must do. Finish. This is you penance."

So I picked up the hammer and the nails, and I finished.

✝

An hour later I went to Hilda. She called the police and the ambulance. He was dead. Gone to heaven. Gone. Gone. Gone.

✝

The priest pulled back, his face awash with amazement. He slowly pulled out of his frozen posture, stiff from the long sit, and raised his right hand over Father Mulcarthy.

"In the name of Jesus Christ, I absolve you of your sins."

He dipped his fingers in the oil and made the sign of the cross over his eyes, ears, nostrils, lips, hands, and feet.

"Through this Holy Unction and His own most tender mercy, may the Lord pardon thee whatever faults thou hast committed by sight, hearing, speech, deed, and thought. Die in grace, in the name of the Father, the Son, and the Holy Spirit. Amen."

The bars slid open, and four uniformed men led Father Mulcarthy down the hall toward the closed door and voltage caution signs. Other men watched him, some silent, some shouting things. Father Mulcarthy spoke clearly, his voice very steady through the concrete hall as he went.

"At six years old, St. Catherine of Siena beat herself on the shoulders with a whip. At eleven, she wore an iron chain round waist. She scourged herself three times daily, slept only half an hour each night, and drank only water. Inspired by St. Ignatius, St. Francis Xavier bound his arms and legs with strings so tightly that his flesh swelled, broke, and covered the strings. His arms nearly required amputation. He took only one meal a day, with sour milk. He slept only two to three hours every night. St. Clare of Montefalco stood barefoot in the snow, reciting the Lord's Prayer one hundred times. St. Arsenius shed so many tears for sins that his eyelashes were forever worn away. St. Novellone walked from Rome to Compostela barefoot, scourging himself all the way. St. Francis de Sales fasted until he was so thin that he "looked more like a skeleton than a living man" beneath his hair shirt. St. Martin de Porres scourged himself three times a night. He wore a chain of iron, a hair shirt, and continually fasted, living on bread and water, with sweet potatoes on Easter, only. He slept on planks, even in the face of malaria. St. Gemma Galgani ate only the communion host, after vigorous fasting. St. Clare founded a community in which all were perpetualy barefoot, slept on the ground, ate no meat, and almost never spoke. Besides this, St. Clare wore a hair shirt and fasted on bread and water, if anything at all, so often that the Bishop of Assisi ordered her to eat at least some bread each day. For fifty years, St. Lupus, the Bishop of Troyes, slept on bare boards and fasted. St. Cunegund, or Kinga, wore a hair shirt. She was also the Queen of Poland. Self-flagellation was public penance in the Middle Ages, and today in Mass we beat our breasts, with the words "Mea Culpa, Mea Culpa, my fault, my fault."

Thomas Peterson was later beatified as a mystic and martyr by the Church. His name still awaits canonization. No official judgment was ever made on the nature and cause of his experiences.

About the Author

Kat Ricker has been published across America and abroad, with awards for journalism, poetry and short stories. Her strength-training articles have appeared in numerous fitness magazines. She holds a master's degree in professional writing from Slippery Rock University.

Kat's vampire story "Everlasting Grace" was named in *The Year's Best Fantasy & Horror: Eighth Annual Collection* and appeared in several publications, including *Terminal Fright*, *Vampires Anonymous*, *Bloodlines*, and *Ladies of Winter: Anthology of the New Gothic*.

Her fright writing has appeared in many publications, including *Black Tears*; *Dark Thirty*; *The Penny Dreadful Review*; *The Sconce*; *Gathering Darkness*; *Samsara*; *Hauntings*; *Bloodlines*; *Eulogy*; *Space and Time*; *Bloodsongs* (Australia); and *Black Tears*, *Nova*, *Roisin Dubh*, and *The Link* in the UK.

Kat's first book, *Something Familiar*, is a collection of poetry and short stories. Her web site is www.MightyKat.net.